Suffolk County Council

GW00633871

FOR SALE

The

Signature of

a Voice

30127 06167655 2

Published by Twenty First Century Publishers Ltd in conjunction with UPSO.

Copyright © Johnny John Heinz 2002.

Johnny John Heinz has asserted his right under the Copyright, Designs and Patents Act 1988 to be identified as the author of this work.

All rights reserved. No part of this work may be reproduced or stored in an information retrieval system (other than for purposes of review) without the prior permission of the copyright holder.

Published in Great Britain, July 2002.

All characters in this book are fictitious, and any resemblance to real persons is pure coincidence.

This book is sold subject to no resale, hiring out, loan or other manner of circulation in form other than this book without the publisher's prior written consent.

ISBN: 1-904433-00-6

Visit our website at www.twentyfirstcenturypublishers.com

The

Signature of

a Voice

The Novel

by

Johnny John Heinz

TF
CP

SUFFOLK COUNTY LIBRARIES & HERITAGE	
H J	09/05/2003
F	£7.99

This book is dedicated to my editorial advisor

Henry Piechoczek

CHAPTER ONE

"This is one major mega-catastrophe." A baritone voice.

"I'll get the Oldsmobile." Almost a falsetto.

"You'll get the what?" boomed the baritone. "There's armed cops outside this goddamn warehouse. You ain't heard the sirens, the megaphone." Once again the megaphone demanded they walk out, hands held high above their heads.

"We gotta get outta here," the falsetto came back, now in a whimper.

"You open that door one inch and they gun you down in one nano-second," boomed the baritone, " and then they storm in here and they take us out." He was fingering his handgun dangerously. A huge man, beefy foreams bowed, a sailor ready to brawl

"Lighten up guys." A melodious voice, a tenor. The tenor jumped lightly off a forklift truck he had been exploring. He moved some packing cases together to improvise seats. "OK, guys. As long as that megaphone keeps it up, we got time to plan. Sit down." The three of them sat on the packing cases and faced one another.

"This is one major screw-up," repeated the baritone.

"You've already said that," responded the tenor. "Anyone worked out what's in here."

"Mostly newsprint," said the falsetto. "I know this place."

"And what are these buildings outside?" asked the tenor.

"Road in, road out, front and back. Left is commercial. Right is residential," the falsetto answered. The megaphone continued with its demands from outside.

"So this is gonna burn well," said the tenor.

"You what?" yelled the baritone. "You crazy? We smoke ourselves out of here? Save them the trouble?"

"OK, guys. Now listen up. This is the plan. We start the fire by one of those vents up there. Smoke will billow out like the whole building's going up. They got no choice. They gotta get the fire department before we roast those turkeys in the neighbouring buildings."

"So what about us?" The falsetto's voice was not that of a man convinced by this logic.

"How many are we?" asked the tenor.

"You know how many we are," roared the baritone. "Three."

"But that's not what they're gonna think with the firepower we packed in the bank and the police cars we shot up in the chase. We had two automobiles. We could be as many as ten. Not for one second do they think we are three guys." The tenor spoke evenly.

"So what the hell kind of difference does that make?" countered the baritone.

"This is what we're gonna do. You two guys are gonna put on those warehouse coats hanging over there. I'm taking you hostage. As soon as we know a fire truck is outside, I'm gonna act like we're smoked out, and come out with guns at your heads, screaming that I'm gonna negotiate for all of us. They're gonna think the rest of us are still in the warehouse, covering me and the hostages."

"So what the hell does that do for us?" the baritone protested.

"This is what the hell it does for us," said the tenor. "We walk past the fire truck. If there's a guy in it, we take him hostage. If there isn't we take the truck. If we can't get the truck started, we grab ourselves our personal fire-fighter. Either way we bang straight through the cops blasting at everything that moves or doesn't move, heads, chests and police cars."

"That is one plan!" The baritone was so taken with it, particularly the blasting at the cops bit, that he even omitted his habitual expletives.

"But where do we go?" asked the falsetto. "Fire trucks don't outrun police cars."

"They're gonna be affected by two things: shock when we storm the fire truck; and lead, as in bullets, when we blast them as three, when they think it's only one of us and two hostages. Also they're gonna be concerned about the guys still in the warehouse, as they wrongly think, packing mighty firepower. They'll probably think the bullets are coming from there. The one thing we did right on this job was to pack the firepower. They'll lose valuable seconds, deciding what to do. Nobody is gonna act without orders in this situation. You got that?"

"I got that," said the falsetto.

"So," the tenor continues, " we strap ourselves in the truck, real tight, like good boys, and head for the shopping mall three blocks down. But we don't want to draw attention to ourselves, so we go in the back way. And when I say the back way, I mean straight through the wall at the back. There's gonna be mayhem when our truck ploughs through the mall: merchandise strewn all over the place; shoppers screaming and running for their vehicles in the parking lot. So we are just three ordinary guys, and like everybody else, we just get the hell outta there. Anyone see any weaknesses?"

Outside Captain Kinley was on the radio updating the situation.

"We got the rear covered. I'm at the front. We got men moving into all the adjoining buildings and on the roofs. No contact yet. Any news on how many they are? What? Someone must have seen something. Dead? Six at the bank. What about our guys? Six cops down! Jesus. Just tell me and we'll storm these bastards right now. No, I don't know if there are any workers inside. Yeah, we're still clearing civilians from the adjoining buildings. Give it ten minutes and everyone will be in position."

He turned to Lieutenant Ralphs.

"This is one bloodbath," said Ralphs.

"Yeah, but I think we've got these guys now, as long as we stay cool," the captain responded. "Jesus, there's smoke coming out of there!"

The captain was straight back on the radio. The deliberation was brief. The adjoining buildings were not yet evacuated. The warehouse was a high fire risk. They had to call in the fire trucks. How the hell was he going to keep the trucks covered? He dare not let the fire take, even to smoke out the occupants of the warehouse.

"Ralphs, we'll need to have the trucks right up by the building, but we've got to cover them. How the hell do we do this? We've got to concentrate our firepower on the door. It cracks open and we have it marked from three angles. We see any guys with guns, we shoot first. No one is going to step out of that door with a gun, unless he plans to use it. Our responsibility is to the fire-fighters."

The dispositions were made and orders given. Captain Kinley was tense, but confident that the men inside the warehouse were under control, trapped with but the front and rear exits for escape, and escape they would have to at some point. He heard the wailing sirens drawing closer, and by now black smoke was billowing out of the building. He could not position police cars between the fire truck and the warehouse, for fear of losing the cars to the fire or blocking the freedom of movement of the fire-fighters. He had to leave the fire truck access, free and clear. It was awkward but manageable, he thought. His men were well positioned, with both cover and a clear shot. One man was in the open to direct the first fire truck into position, another truck would come to the rear of the warehouse and two more served as back up.

As the first truck was moving into position the warehouse pedestrian entry door creaked open a couple of inches. The officers took aim. A grey glad arm snaked out, dangling a white cloth. Then the door swung fully open to reveal a warehouseman clad in a grey coat, arms at his sides.

"Hold your fire," screamed Kinley. "Hands above your head."

The warehouseman raised his arms and a second warehouse-man stepped forward beside him. And it was then that Kinley saw a third man behind them, a gun to the head of each.

"I'm covered from inside, so hold your frigging bullets," shouted the tenor. "We want to negotiate. One false move and the first of these two workers gets his brains blown out. If I go down they both go down." The warehouse door gaped open behind him to reveal an emplacement of packing cases with gun barrels poking out.

Kinley was experienced and knew he must take the tension out of the standoff, lure them into negotiations and keep them sweet. With civilians still in the surrounding buildings, there was too much at stake, particularly after the mayhem that had taken place in the bank and during the chase. It will be even better if they come right out into the open, he thought, and sure enough they were moving towards him. Apart from one man in the cab, the fire-fighters had jumped out to start work. They now ran to take cover as beckoned by the police on their side of the truck.

From the cover of his position behind a police car, Kinley started to speak through the megaphone. And this was enough to give the tenor direction. Kinley, commander of his troops, took the very first shot through the head. In less than two seconds the trio, with a barrage of gunfire in all directions, were up in the cab of the fire truck, lying on the floor with a gun to the stomach of the driver, and clear instructions in his ear. In the hail of bullets no one appreciated what was happening or where the gunfire came from until the truck roared off. After fifty yards the driver rolled out with a bullet in the stomach.

"Cover the building," Ralphs screamed, as he looked around for a team to chase the fire truck. At least only one of the bad guys was getting away. "Get HQ on the radio. Get the ambulances. He had to establish who had gone down apart from Kinley. He had to keep the building covered. And the fire! Despite total confusion, the second fire truck moved up into position, and the fire-fighters set their operation in motion. Ralphs screamed to his men to get the wounded clear and pulled in the three men closest to him.

"We've gotta go in there," he yelled to the two officers next to him. "Come on." They ran to the corner of the warehouse and then along to where the door was set in the wall.

"OK, you guys," Ralphs whispered. "You poke your guns round the door and blast away at them, but keep it high. I'm gonna roll in underneath their return fire. I've got ten feet to the packing cases, and then I don't know what, but I've gotta do it. Wish me luck." They reached round the doorway firing rapidly and Ralphs dived for the cases, rolling beneath the gun barrels. He grabbed the first barrel, yanked and the gun came free. He grabbed the second, and then realised there was no return fire.

"Hold your fire," he screamed. He lay there in silence, as in no gunfire. Gingerly he pushed a packing case aside. No one was there. Keeping behind the cases he looked around the warehouse. There was no movement.

"Come on out," he shouted. He saw that the fire had taken hold only on the far left corner of the warehouse at the top, and it dawned on him that they had been tricked. He stood up and ran to the back of the warehouse. No one. Behind the rolls of newsprint. No one.

"It's all clear," he shouted back to his two men. "Get the fire truck in here. They'll have this blaze under control in minutes."

Relieved at gaining control of the warehouse, devastated by the loss of Captain Kinley, Ralphs began to radio in his report, still in possession of himself, adrenalin still flowing. Even as he spoke the emergency call came through from the police cars that had given chase to the fire truck. They were at the shopping mall, and needed back up right now. Giving swift instructions to secure the warehouse, he took off himself and reached the mall in less than a minute.

Those seconds of confusion at the warehouse had given the stolen fire truck a lead. The tenor had decided that they would manoeuvre the truck backwards into the mall to limit injury to themselves. The body of the truck had smashed through the wall into rows of shelves in the store, but the lower speed in reverse gear resulted in the cab being stuck outside. The three simply jumped out of the cab and walked around the corner, where they boarded a municipal bus that had just pulled up at the stop. The bus driver pulled away unaware of the chaos that the fire truck had caused in the mall, fortunately limited only to physical damage. As soon as he arrived, Ralphs sealed off the area, but they quickly ascertained that there were no warehousemen, no hostages and no one resembling the occupants of the fire truck. It was a dead end.

***

John Ralphs, thirty-three year old police lieutenant, personal friend of Captain Kinley, pushed open the door of his apartment three hours later. His wife, Jennifer, rushed forward and threw her arms around him, tears streaming down her cheeks.

"I saw it on the news, John. I can't believe it." The words came through her sobs.

"I was there, Jenny," he said. " I was there. It only hits me now. We lost eight men today and four are in hospital. They're all my friends, were all my friends. There was nothing we could do. We chased these guys and they just blasted the hell out of us and everything else. They rammed a fire truck right into a crowded shopping mall. They set off a fire that could have burnt down a whole apartment block. They gunned down four people in the bank."

"Who are they?" She shuddered.

"So far all I've got is the sight of three of them in those few seconds when they left the warehouse, and the sound of that one guy's voice."

CHAPTER TWO

The Herald and Courier

THE PEACE OF OUR TOWN SHATTERED

We are in mourning today for the tragic loss of thirteen of our citizens. Few of you will be unaware by now of the dreadful events that shook our town yesterday morning: eight police officers lost their lives in the line of duty; three bank staff were treacherously gunned down; and one innocent bystander died in the gun battle. Four police officers and one fire-fighter lie in hospital with serious wounds.

At eleven a.m. the first of the gang members, brandishing an automatic weapon, entered and sought to take control of the bank branch on Main Street. He was overpowered by the manager and two employees who pinned him to the ground face down. The alarms sounded and within three minutes the first police officers arrived outside the bank.

From this point events are unclear. It seems that another member of the gang, also in the crowded banking hall, went out to greet the officers and advise them that all was under control. As they entered the hall, he shot them in the back. At the same time another gang member, also in the hall, opened fire, killing the bank manager, his two staff pinning down the prisoner, and a customer. The freed gangster rose to his feet screaming to everyone in the hall to lie flat and close their eyes.

No eyewitnesses were able to describe his appearance, but several recall his very high-pitched voice.

Outside the building the next police car arrived and both officers were gunned down in their vehicle by the gangster on the street.

At this point it appears the gang aborted their heist and decided to flee. A patrol vehicle arriving at the scene pursued a red Oldsmobile that pulled away from the bank. A Chevrolet swung out behind the patrol vehicle and in a hail of bullets both police officers died in their patrol vehicle.

Having lost six officers already, incredibly the police hemmed in the two escaping vehicles and forced the gang to take refuge in a warehouse on Gridle Street. As the police were securing the area, fire broke out in the warehouse, which adjoins both residential and commercial property. The Fire Department arrived in minutes, but another gun battle ensued. Captain Kinley who had heroically led his men against this brutal gang and trapped them was fatally shot. There was confusion about hostages being taken, and in this confusion three of the gang took off in a fire truck, inflicting a stomach wound on the driver. Mayhem was narrowly avoided when, minutes later, they rammed the truck through the rear wall of Madison's Shopping Mall, destroying much of the store. While the truck escaped the police stormed the empty warehouse. None of the gang, which may have numbered as many as ten, was apprehended.

Our sympathies go out to the families of those for whom we mourn.

While we are in mourning today, questions will be asked later. Why was no one apprehended? Why did the police not stop the escaping fire truck? Was there a catastrophic breakdown of control after Captain Kinley's fatal shooting?

Eyewitness interviews on centre pages.

Jenny looked down blankly at the front page of the newspaper lying on her kitchen table. It was so awful to see it in black and white. Like many businesses in town, hers had stayed closed today as a mark of respect. She looked up as the entry door opened.

"John!" He stood framed in the doorway. His normally erect posture was slumped. The gleam in his blue eyes had been replaced by dull sunken look. His usually fresh features were drawn and haggard.

"I've been suspended," he said.

"Why?" Jenny asked.

"Just when they need me to go after these bastards. We've lost eight men. And they want to investigate me, to investigate what happened."

"What do you mean, John?"

"They're saying they don't know if I did my job. They're saying the Fire Department think I risked their men. I let the runaway fire truck ram the mall, and god knows what else."

"But that's not what happened, John. You told me last night."

"I told you what I saw, Jenny. Others saw it differently. The people taking the decisions weren't even there."

"I don't understand, John."

"Neither do I, Jenny. I've been running it through my mind on the way back. I was in charge for no more that four minutes. Kinley went down in the firefight that lasted maybe three of four seconds. It's not like in the movies or in detective stories. In the real world, like yesterday, a firefight lasts seconds. I focused on the warehouse, where I could see the guns, and where we thought there were maybe as many as nine bad guys. The warehouse was on fire. I had to get in there. That was about thirty seconds. I spent no more than a minute in the warehouse, maybe fifteen seconds reporting back, and then within a minute we were at the mall. I secured the situation instantly there – everyone was co-operating and no one was panicking, despite what had happened. Four minutes, Jenny, just four minutes. After that it was just a question of checking everyone out and cleaning up."

"So why are you suspended?"

"Some of the guys say they could have stopped the truck. Ross thinks I stopped him shooting the guy with the hostages after Kinley was hit. The Fire Department say the police hindered them in tackling the blaze and risked the driver of the fire truck unnecessarily. It's a mess."

They looked at each other and realised that this was not there real concern. They were both thinking of the friends they had lost yesterday. In a lower voice John Ralphs continued. "Jenny, what happened yesterday was real. What is happening today is bureaucracy. From the moment I took charge yesterday not one life was lost. I risked everything going into that warehouse, to make sure of that. Whatever they may say now, I had to do that. I could not have saved Kinley or the men who went before him, or the officer who went down with him. If I had stopped the fire truck, maybe the driver would be dead, rather than wounded, and probably more officers would be dead." She took his hand.

"I know, John," she said.

Ross came by that evening to fill John in on developments. They had trained together, worked together and if John was technically ranked higher, they both recognised this as being through chance and not ability. After the initial greeting Jenny left them to it, and John poured them both a Jack Daniels. Ross sat back and relaxed. Close to six feet tall, his stature was similar to John's. He too had blue eyes and boyish looks, though not today.

"Hey, John, you're not looking so good," Ross opened.

"And you look even worse, buddy. So what gives on the case?" John enquired.

"Nothing. We know nothing more than you already know. We don't even know what they planned in the bank," Ross responded.

"Do we know how many they were?" John asked.

"Apart from the three you and I saw, the rest just vanished," Ross replied.

"I need to work on this, Ross."

"I know you do. The bosses have to do their thing, I guess. This is the worst atrocity that has ever happened in this town. It's their job to hedge their bets right now," Ross explained.

"Why do they need to do that?" John asked.

"Well," Ross continued, "to contain any screw-ups, real or perceived. I didn't see the crime scene the way you did, John. My statement, it seems, was not in your favour."

"Well, what did you see then, Ross?"

"I smelt smoke from the warehouse. I saw three guys come out. I saw Kinley stand up where I was crouched beside him. I saw him lift the megaphone to his lips. Then a bang and he was down. I leapt up covered in Kinley's blood, wiped my eyes clear and saw weapons drawn out of the pockets of the pretend hostages. I drew my gun and got a clear line on them. You stopped me from shooting, John."

"I did?"

"You raised your right arm at waist height and turned the palm towards me, John. I had a clear sight. I saw the guys pull their guns, and I was going to shoot, until you stopped me."

"I don't recall doing that, Ross, and if I did, it wasn't to stop you."

"But you did stop me, John," Ross persisted.

"I was focused on the warehouse," John continued, "at stopping the nine remaining guys. Then when I saw a hostage climbing into the truck with a gun in his hand, I guessed he had overpowered the bad guy and was taking cover in the truck from the guys in the warehouse, who it seemed to me were blasting in every direction."

"But you see, John, that isn't what happened. They've been interviewing the officers who were present and getting all kinds of different stories. The main story that's coming out is that you heroically, single-handedly stormed an empty warehouse, while the only guys who could lead us to the gang drove off, god help us, in a fire truck."

"That's after the event, Ross. That's once we all know what happened. Back then I saw one bad guy, two hostages, and one warehouse full of bad guys with heavy weapons, a warehouse on fire, threatening neighbouring buildings."

Ross eyed John steadily. "Unfortunately, reality went on to undermine your position, John. Unfortunately, I saw it differently at the time and told them what I saw, before I had any idea there would be an investigation. What I saw is what actually happened. I saw one bad guy and two hostages turn into three very bad guys who had killed my captain. I saw those guys steal a fire truck that was supposed to be putting out a fire. I saw one warehouse totally under our control with all exits covered. No one else could get out. I saw the opportunity to shoot and apprehend, dead or alive, three bad guys, who are now free. When you stopped me, I had to assume you had a better plan, and followed orders."

"I get your point, Ross. But we didn't know. I had to do the best I could. Judge the best I could. I was in control for just four minutes. In a critical situation there were no further fatalities."

"A critical four minutes, John. Fact is the bad guys got away, bad guys who killed eight police officers and civilians. Fact is the Fire Department went apeshit."

John looked at Ross and for the first time reality began to dawn on him. This was a real investigation and his, Lieutenant John Ralph's, actions were being questioned. He began to have doubts about his own judgement at the scene. Ross saw these thoughts developing and stopped him stone dead.

"John," Ross said, "let me be clear about this. It just happens that what I saw proved to be true after the event. Luck was on my side. You *knew* there were hostages and you were looking at the warehouse for the source of gunfire, so you did not see what I saw. That's all. Your hand movement was probably an unconscious warning to me to get down that I misinterpreted. That's why you don't remember it."

"You know what I want more than anything, Ross. I want to get on this case and nail these bastards. And you know what? From what you've just said, I don't think that's going to happen." John leant back in his seat, deflated.

"I don't think we would be on this case anyway, John. It's too big for us."

***

It took Lieutenant John Ralphs less than a week to work out that the luxury of not having to get out of bed to go to work was no luxury, that the luxury of being paid to stay at home was no luxury, and that the freedom to do whatever he wanted was no freedom for him. What he wanted to do he could not do, so long as he was suspended. He went out: he came home. He tried to read: he couldn't concentrate. He watched TV: there was nothing to watch. He would see friends, but friends were at work. He worked out at the gym: the gym was empty. He went to the shopping mall, but there was nothing he needed to buy. He stuck his head in a bar – empty. On the fifth day he called Ross on the phone and learnt that there was no progress on any front, least of all on the investigation into him.

By the time Jenny came home in the evening of the fifth day, a course of action was beginning to form in his head. What the police had to go on was forensics: bullets, weapons and the abandoned stolen cars. Ross had given him one snippet of information. A very realistic false nose had been found on the floor of the bank, so the gang had been disguised. This meant that even the brief view of the three men coming out of the warehouse was unlikely to be of value. Meanwhile he was the police, but they were paying him to sit at home doing nothing.

Why should he not undertake some investigations on his own? There is nothing illegal in that, he had nothing to do and he knew as much as anyone else. He needed someone to talk this through with. He would talk it through with Jenny. Maybe he could also get Ross interested. When it came down to it, they all wanted to nail the bastards. Even though he was suspended, surely they would appreciate any valuable private assistance he could lend. Maybe he could even do things in an unofficial capacity that they would not want to do officially. The idea was beginning to excite him, and the boredom of the last five days was slipping away.

Jenny came in, bouncy as usual. The pall hanging over the beginning of the week was lifting. Her shoulder-length blonde hair bounced with her, like in the commercials, blending with her pale complexion and chestnut eyes. She was smiling, wanting her cheerfulness to spill over onto John. She was surprised by his good spirits and new enthusiasm. Over the course of the evening he went through his thoughts with her. Now they were sitting over a bourbon.

"What it comes down to Jenny, all I have, is that voice. The sound of those words is taped onto my consciousness: *We want to negotiate. One false move and the first of these two workers gets his brains blown out. If I go down they both go down.* Three full sentences Jenny. You know, it's like when you answer the phone: you don't have to ask your friends who it is, mostly they don't even say. I'll know that voice anywhere."

"But John, we don't know, where he comes from, if he's local or out of town. We don't even know what they planned."

"And you know the other thing I might recognise," John continued, "is the way he moves. I've got nothing to lose, Jenny. I have time on my hands. What we have to do is work out how to do the search."

Jenny thought about this. "You know, in the old days you could have been a telephone operator. I'm brainstorming, John."

With John it sparked: "That's fantastic, Jenny. What's the equivalent today? It's even better. It's telephone sales. I can call any godamm number I like. I don't even need them to listen to me. I can do such a pathetic screwed up sales pitch that they just tell me to go away, relieved to get me off the line and think no more of it. The only problem is the women answer the phones."

Jenny laughed. "John, the police do not always lead the way in being politically correct, do they? Maybe he's not married."

"You know what I'm going to do. I'm going to meet Ross at lunchbreak tomorrow, and we're going to work out a system for generating numbers to call. We'll draw up a profile of who the guy might be and match it to telephone numbers. This is truly amazing. I've been thinking about this all afternoon and the best I could come up with was to be a taxi driver or a bartender, people who get to hear strangers speak."

John was sitting in Juanita's eyeing the menu, when Ross came in, and took a seat opposite. After the usual jokes about the menu, Ross turned to the subject.

"You know, since we talked last night I checked out a few things on the department's computer and did a couple of calculations," Ross said.

"And what did you come up with?" John asked.

"Well," a smile was playing on Ross's lips, "we reckon that if you keep it down to twenty seconds per call, you could poll the whole US in, say, about one hundred and fifty years. The problem is, the way we see it, that even if you get lucky, and get him half way through, you'd still be dead by then. This is real traditional gumshoe stuff, John."

"So this it a screwed up plan, is it?" John looked miserable.

"As luck would have it," Ross continued, "my brother, Chris, was round last night. He's in software development. He was excited. Said this could be a totally new idea worth looking at. He suggested you show up at his place at two today, after we've had lunch."

John pulled up outside a smoked glass building with parking spaces in front. He entered the foyer and a porter called up for Chris. They introduced themselves and Chris took John through to a meeting room on the ground level. Chris jumped straight in without any preliminaries.

"I'll tell you what I think, John. In my business we spend our time working out ways to shape reams of data into meaningful form. When we have a good system we sell it as often as we can. Now tell me. You know this guy's voice?"

"I'd recognise it anytime, Chris."

"Then forget this telephone sales crap. All you've got to do is have him answer the phone. When my wife says *hello* I know it's her. I don't ask her to speak three sentences, which is what I gather you are working off," Chris explained.

"You're right. I hadn't seen it like that, Chris."

"So we're going to do four things. One: do a profile of the guy. Two: use the profile to eliminate telephone numbers we don't need to call. Three: automate the calling process on a PC. Four: evaluate the results. We will eliminate most calls with an automatic process on the PC and what is left will be recorded for you to listen to."

"Jesus, Chris. Can we do that? You mean the PC makes all the calls, sifts through them and I just listen to the likely ones."

"You've got it, John. If we had the guy's voice taped, you wouldn't even have to do that. We'd just wait for an acoustic match. In this case we have to use you for that bit. Think you can do it?" Chris asked, grinning.

"You bet, Chris."

"OK, John. We want to do the tightest profile of the guy possible. It doesn't matter if we get it wrong, because we can always come back and change it, but with a tight profile, you'll find we have surprisingly few calls to make. Use your gut feel, John."

"So I draw up a profile?" John asked.

"Yeah, and get Ross to help. He was there too. Start with the easy bits. He wasn't a woman, right? Did he sound educated? Do bank robbers live in the country or towns? Would someone come in from New York to plan a raid in our little town? What's his likely age range? For example, we could eliminate all the phone numbers which have been in place for more than five years if he was, say, twenty-five. But you guys are policemen. You know all this better than me. You get the gist?"

"This is fantastic, Chris. And I thought we were brainstorming last night."

"Bring, me a profile tomorrow, John. But do one thing. Get

hold of a keyboard. You know, one of those Jap things. Switch it to *human voice* and try and get me an acoustic range. Listen to some CD's with male singers, and try and get one in the same range. That way I'll write into the program that any voice outside that range is eliminated immediately. And, John, some of those guys who died were my friends. I'm gonna have a PC here in the office make the calls and bill it to software development." John left the building walking on air, suddenly glad that he was suspended. No way would they have followed up this lead back in the Police Department.

CHAPTER THREE

When José Carreras, Plácido Domingo and Luciano Pavarotti performed in Rome on 7 July 1990, they probably did not consider the assistance they would be providing the Police Department a decade later. It was this CD of the three tenors that John sent across to Chris the next day for the acoustic profile, to set bounds to the range of frequencies of the voice they were seeking.

As Chris had suggested, they started with a very tight profile that listed numerous characteristics including that the raider lived within ten miles of the bank. This profile generated very few telephone numbers, just over five hundred. With the software ready for testing three days later, they chose to call between seven and ten in the evening. Including redials for busy numbers, it took just under two hours to complete the process. Just five calls of the five hundred plus were unsuccessful in getting a voice. There were no voices that fitted the profile for John to listen to.

Over the next few days they progressively widened the profile and voice matches began to come in. Chris also introduced a system for second calls where females had answered the phone in the hope of catching a male voice second time. If the townsfolk were tiring of unsolicited calls, they did not show it. Mostly the PC cut off as soon as a match failed on the first syllable. They were soon extending their geographical reach and accessing telephone directories outside the immediate area, and they added in the hours of seven to eight in the morning for making calls, giving them four hours of calling a day. Chris decided to speed it up further by hooking up to a second telephone line. They had thought the overload would be on John listening to voices, but it turns out that there aren't so many tenors around, or at least not tenors who answer the phone.

In a farmhouse forty miles outside town three men had gathered. Bill Hadley was just bringing beers up for them from the cellar, when the phone went.

"Hello," Jim Duggan answered in his shrill, almost female voice. Then he hung up.

"Who was that?" Bill asked.

"No one," Jim replied.

"What do you mean no one?"

"They just hung up, if there was anyone there to start with," Jim whined.

"Look. I answer my phone. You got that." Bill's anger came through, sharpening his usual melodious tone, a tenor. He turned to the third of the men from the warehouse, from the bank raid.

"Give me a beer," commanded Bob Mitchell, the baritone, in his usual booming tone, matching his bulk.

"The way I see it," Bill said, "handing each of them a beer, "is we need cash and that means we need a new plan."

"I lost three weapons," Bob stated. "I need weapons as well as cash. I feel naked."

Bill interrupted. "I was thinking we should go north this time after the bloodbath down south, but I've changed my mind. The last thing they will expect is that we do the same bank."

"I like that," agreed, Jim, the falsetto.

"Yeah, it was real fun last time. Count me in," boomed Bob.

"I say, let's hit 'em now, while they're down. Next week. Agreed." Bill looked round to nods of agreement, from his accomplices, the contrast of thin, whining Jim and beefy Bob, loud booming, expansive.

It was three days later that the fallibility of Chris's software resulted in the breakthrough. It had mistaken Jim Duggan's sex, confused by his shrill voice. The second call, made when females answered the first, was automatically programmed and yielded: "Hello, Bill Hadley…No, I don't need tableware." An acoustic match, as in this case, triggered a telephone sales pitch to catch an extra line, if possible, and it had. The next morning John was running through his routine listening schedule, when he stopped dead at the third voice: *Hello, Jim Duggan…No, I don't need tableware*. In his head he heard the echo: *We want to negotiate. One false move and the first of these two workers gets his brains blown out. If I go down they both go down.* John did not even bother to replay it. He called Ross instantly.

Later that day Ross climbed the stairs to John Ralph's apartment. If he felt deflated, he had no idea of how John was going to feel. He rang and Jenny answered.

"What's wrong, Ross. You look like you've been…I don't know what," she said.

"Is John here? Please join us too, Jenny." Ross suggested as, John came out of the lounge, beaming.

"Hey, Ross, come on in. Have a drink. Good news. I can't believe it was so quick. Chris is amazing." They sat down and John produced a couple of cold beers.

Ross began, "So you're sure about the voice, John?"

"I am 100% certain," John replied. "No doubt whatsoever."

"I heard him just like you did, and I would have agreed with you." Ross acknowledged.

"What do you mean *would have?*" John's surprise showed.

"I saw him in the flesh today. They sent me to interview him as one of the guys who saw him at the warehouse. I heard that same voice," Ross continued.

"So you've taken him in?" John queried, but a touch nervously.

"He lives forty miles north on a farm. I met him in his office twenty miles north. I couldn't have recognised him physically, but it sounded exactly like the guy. Outside I had armed back up. But listen, John. He's an investment advisor. Quite a successful one. So I asked him where he was on the morning of the raid. Outside the office probably, he says. Most mornings I am."

"It's sounding good," John commented.

"But it isn't," Ross continued. "He pulls out his diary and says he'll check. And right there he has two appointments in his office, at eleven and at eleven thirty, i.e. when we were at the warehouse".

"Does he have a secretary to corroborate this?" John asked.

"Only in the afternoons. He says it's the nature of the business. So I ask for his card index and I take down the names of the guys he was seeing. They were both local, so we went round to see them, Bob Mitchell and Jim Duggan. They both swear separately that they were in his office, although Mitchell had left by the time Duggan arrived."

"I don't believe it," John spluttered.

"I didn't either, John, but it's true. We'll have to go for another voice match to another guy. First, he doesn't look like he's the type to rob banks, and then he has two cast iron alibis." Jenny, in the background, sat transfixed. Had it all been for nothing?

"Did you tell them about the voice?" she asked.

"No," Ross responded, "and by the way, our seniors are not very enthusiastic about this voice thing. They say that even if we find the bad guy, it doesn't prove anything. There are plenty of crooks that we know are crooks but can't touch."

Forty miles north in Hadley's farmhouse they were in good spirits.

Bob Mitchell roared with laughter. "I told them I only spent ten minutes with you, because I had to get into town to go to the bank. Then when I get there half an hour later, I find everything closed up. So I decide to go to the shopping mall and find that all cordoned off. Then he asks me how long I've known you, and I tell him you are the most serious, the most sober-headed investment advisor in the area and that you were recommended to me by the bank."

"I like that," Bill Hadley said. "A nice bit of authenticity about the bank. OK, boys, this is looking good. We'll go in on Tuesday and hit the place, this time successfully. I'm buying an air ticket to New York. I'll have someone fly for me and give me the boarding card stubs as well as a hotel receipt on my credit card. That way, if necessary, I can prove I was in New York." With that they moved on to the planning of the raid.

It niggled Bill Hadley, in the back of his mind, how it was that the police had got onto him so fast. They had prepared for this eventuality with well-rehearsed alibis, but there was still no clue as to the source of the police's lead. I'm going to have to find out about this, he thought, and then do something about it.

***

A red pick-up truck cruised along Main Street. The back was loaded up with lawn mowers and gardening equipment, and in the front sat three men, similar in stature but different in appearance from the three at the farmhouse. Traffic was light, as they pulled over to the kerb immediately opposite the bank. It was Tuesday, eleven a.m.

Inside the bank staff and customers alike were nervous. It is absurd, but that is the way people think: they are acutely aware of the earlier disaster, even though it is obvious that the same bank is not going to be hit at the same time on the same day just three weeks later. There were five staff at the counters, but just three customers. Then a blast of automatic gunfire shattered glass, furniture and walls. Part of the ceiling crashed to the floor, and everyone dived flat to the ground for cover. This time there was no an attempt to go for the alarm. The staff were frozen.

"Make this quick and stay alive," a deep voice boomed, followed by a second burst of gunfire. Bullets ricocheted off the walls.

"I have two garbage sacks here, which I am sliding into teller positions one and two. I'm giving you twenty seconds to fill them from when I start counting. Now move, because if I shoot again, it's with human targets and I don't count many in here to choose from. One…two…"

Thirty seconds later Bob Mitchell stepped out of the bank carrying a holdall with the garbage bags inside and turned left to the side street where Bill Hadley was parked. Opposite the bank Jim Duggan pushed the gear selector of the pick-up into drive, set the steering to take it straight along Main Street, stepped out with a goodbye wave to the driver and slammed the door. In the driver's seat sat a tailor's dummy, fully clothed, strategically kitted out with blood and body parts from a slaughtered pig. Whatever happened to the pick-up, and some kind of crash would be inevitable, it would be a valuable decoy, costing time for any would-be pursuers. Jim strolled across Main Street into the side street to join Bill Hadley and they were away, turning left on Main Street and heading north. There were no sirens and no pursuit. Outside the bank all was calm and quiet, for the moment.

"Well, this won't make us rich," Bill said.

"True, but picking up twenty grand before lunch is OK by me." Bob gave a deep booming laugh. "This time there was only one guy, me, and as far as they know I didn't even figure last time."

"Hang on. There's someone chasing us," yelled Bill, as glancing in his rear view mirror, he saw a vehicle approaching rapidly. Jim Duggan prepared his weapons. A Corvette screamed past at around a hundred miles an hour.

"Jesus! Just some joker in a hurry," Jim squeaked from the back seat, "but I've got his number just in case we need to feed in any information on unusual behaviour."

Sitting at home eating a sandwich, John Ralphs flicked on the news at one o'clock. He stared in disbelief as the newsflash came up: another bank raid, same place, same day, same time. They're smart, the thought. That we would not have guessed. He reached for the phone to call Ross, but stopped himself. Ross would be busy. The phone rang. It was Ross.

"John, we're clutching at straws." Ross was clearly under high stress. "There's nothing to go on, except a wrecked pick-up truck, stolen from some contract gardeners. There's going to be a big meeting to look for links between the two raids, and I think you are going to be invited.

***

The Herald and Courier

WHO ARE THESE EVIL MEN?

Fellow citizens, at eleven a.m. yesterday, three weeks to the day, three weeks to the very hour and minute of the day, these evil men were back in our town. This time their bank heist was successful, if small, and mercifully there were no casualties. Who are these callous creatures that visit their horror upon us as we still mourn our lost friends?

At exactly eleven a.m. a large man entered the bank branch on Main Street, firing an automatic weapon indiscriminately. Within less than a minute he had forced two of the three cashiers to load the cash they held behind the counter into bags and was gone. No one dared move for some minutes, remembering the events of three weeks ago. Then the alarm was activated.

In a bizarre twist, shortly after eleven, a red pick-up truck, loaded with horticultural equipment veered off Main Street and ploughed into Duncan's Hardware Store. The store manager called the ambulance service immediately as the driver looked in a bad way. And this is bizarre: there was no driver, just a dummy stuffed with animal body parts.

The police have connected the bank robbery and the pick-up truck, which was stolen. The police appeal for witnesses of yesterday's events to come forward. There have been reports of a vehicle heading north at high speed shortly after the robbery. The police seek information to identify the vehicle and its occupants.

Once again, like *déjà vu*, Jenny was sitting in her kitchen looking down at the newspaper, an article about a bank raid. This time John was there with her.

"They have nothing, Jenny. Not from first time and not yet from this time," John was saying.

"They have your *voice*, John," she said.

"But it was wrong," he answered. "I was mistaken and that's it. If I was mistaken once, what hope is there for a second match?"

"I can't get this one idea out of my head," she said.

"What idea?" he asked, still mournful, dejected.

"Well, I wasn't at the crime scene, the warehouse," she explained, "so I just have this abstract image of one man and two hostages. I don't visualise them. They're just an idea."

"And?" John was not following her yet.

"And I wasn't at the interview with the man with the voice, the investment advisor. One man with two alibis." She looked at him. "Do you see what I mean?"

"I don't think I do, Jenny," he answered.

"Listen, John. One man with two hostages, but they weren't hostages. One man with two alibis…"

"You mean," John started, but she interrupted him.

"Yes, John. Two alibis from two men. Three men at the warehouse. What are these alibis, John? Are they like the hostages, fake?"

The problem was that they had no evidence. In fact, the *evidence* was against them in the form of sworn alibis. They took stock of what they had: one voice identification, assuming they had it right, which was in question. It had not been accepted at the police meeting John had been invited to in the morning. Jenny pulled out the first newspaper article from three weeks ago and the reference to the shrill voice of the raider in the banking hall caught her eye. Several of the witnesses in the banking hall must have heard it. She proposed that they get the voices of Duggan and Mitchell on tape and try it on a couple of the witnesses, to see if they have any sense of recognition for either of them. Then she proposed that she should pose as an investor and visit Hadley. They could put together a script and try to prompt him into using the exact words as had been used at the warehouse, when he came out with the hostages. They could dub that onto a tape to get the words in the right order and try it on Ross, and if he responded positively, a couple of the other officers who were present. It might not be evidence, but maybe it could point the finger.

They agreed to work on both approaches and John's despondency began to lift, as he saw constructive work to be done, but he was outclassed by Jenny's enthusiasm. She obtained the numbers from the directory. She put the phone down on Mitchell as soon as she heard his deep baritone. She could not help but give a little gasp when she heard Duggan's shrill voice on the line. She played him along for a bit asking for an unknown Philippa, and then put the phone down beaming. They were on target. Now they had to prove it.

CHAPTER FOUR

Bill Hadley was an investment advisor, but not a very successful one. The problem was finding the clients. If they wanted to work with him, they did not seem to have enough money, and if they had money, it always seemed to be tied up elsewhere. Apart from that, since his divorce, he had been looking for a bit of excitement.

Planning bank raids in his spare time at the office had amused him. It was just a game he played to fill time. One day going over a plan with Bob Mitchell, he had thought Bob was joking when he said he would join *the gang* to get an opportunity to try out his weapons for real. It had become serious with Jim Duggan. Bill had known Jim for years, a weird guy, well known as a kind of local historian. Jim knew all the old stories about the town, where the saloons were, the brothels, which families feuded and so on. When Jim joined him and Bob for a poker game one evening and heard them running over the plans for a bank raid, Jim did not for a moment doubt they were serious. When he realised they weren't serious, Jim became angry, telling them it was a recent phenomenon not to raid banks and they should get back to their roots.

The discussion developed and the truth became clear: the truth was that none of them had any qualms about robbing banks. In fact, they wanted to do it. They would plan meticulously, arm themselves to the hilt and execute ruthlessly. This would be their trademark. Any casualties would be collateral damage as far as they were concerned. As Bob put it, weapons weren't built for pussycats.

Bill did not often get calls from prospective clients, but neither was it completely out of the ordinary. When Jean Galloway called up, he said he could squeeze her in the next day in the afternoon for an introductory meeting, if that suited her, which it did. Now he sat there waiting. She was not on time, but that did not matter. He was reliving last Tuesday's success.

Jenny, under the alias of Jean Galloway, was on time, but she was outside in her Buick, suffering a last minute attack of nerves. Back in her kitchen it had all seemed so easy, and it probably was for John, a trained police officer. Now she was about to enter the office of someone she believed to be a brutal, merciless, ruthless killer. She was about to embark on a game of cat-and-mouse with him, and he was supposed to be the mouse. This man who gunned down innocent bystanders, police officers and shot a fire-fighter in the belly, was supposed to be the mouse, and she innocent, bouncy, friendly Jenny, the cat. She was not sure she could do this, and her hand trembled as she read through her scripts yet again. Finally, she focused on the friends they had lost, pulled herself together and stepped out of the car.

"Mrs Galloway, do come in. Please have a seat. It is my pleasure to greet you here today." She could not have been more shocked, as the melodious voice of Hadley washed gently around her. She took a place opposite his desk and was involuntarily finding she liked him. Gone were her nerves, gone was the sharp edge of her tension, and she relaxed into his gentle questioning. But she was still aware of the tape running in her handbag, seeking every now and then to elicit the responses from him that she needed, the words of the man at the warehouse. At least he had no suspicions, she thought, as the meeting progressed. She glanced at her watch. More than an hour had elapsed, although it seemed much less. The meeting wound to an end. She left a phone number and promised to call him, after she had had time to consider her financial position, and thanked him for his advice. As soon as he had shown her to the door, Hadley moved back to his desk and picked up the phone.

"Bob, its Bill. Get Duggan and come over right now. I'm worried."

Ross joined John and Jenny that evening, as usual in the kitchen. She told them about the meeting with Hadley that she had taped. She talked about her struggle to prompt him to say the right words, the key words they had heard at the warehouse. There was an hour's worth of tape in which to find the individual words that made up: *We want to negotiate. One false move and the first of these two workers gets his brains blown out. If I go down they both go down.* It took forty-five minutes of the tape before they had been able to tick off each of the words on the list, but they were not sure how it would work out with the intonation once they had strung all the words together. Ross said he would drop the tape off to Chris on the way back, and see if Chris could do something with it, by recording it onto their computer and editing it. In the meantime, both he and John were pretty well convinced that this was their man. The voice just sounded exactly right.

Duggan had not been available that afternoon, so it was not until the evening that Bill Hadley, Bob Mitchell and Jim Duggan met together at Hadley's farmhouse.

"So what made me suspicious," Hadley was saying, "is that she would be following the conversation normally, and then every now and then it was like she was reading her lines and she would ask me a question. Towards the end of the meeting, it struck me that whenever this happened, she would glance down at her handbag."

"So what could she want?" Duggan squawked.

"You tell me," Hadley replied. He fixed them both with a steady eye. "Anything strange happen to you two guys." Silence. They shook their heads. "Any strange calls? Any calls from strangers?"

"I got one woman," Duggan said, "asking for some woman I don't know, but I cut her off pretty quick."

"OK, Duggan, you try this number. See if it's her." Hadley

passed Jean Galloway's number across. Duggan entered the number. The number did not go through. It did not exist.

"Let's think about this," Hadley said. "She gives me a dud number. That means she can't ever come back to me. Right?"

Bob Mitchell had been sitting back. Intellectual activity was not his great strength, but this seemed so obvious to him, that he explained: "She's probably made a teeny weeny mistake, reversed a digit. Anyone can. That way, if she wants to come back to you and you query the number, she takes a look and says, ooh, I'm so sorry and so on."

"Good one, Bob," Bill thanked him. " I like it, so let's take a look."

After a good deal of examination and comparison with numbers in the area, they came up with five options. Duggan set about trying the numbers. On the second attempt, a female voice answered, and it sounded right to Duggan. Duggan put the phone down and whistled. "That's her." Again the solution was easy for Mitchell.

"She's on to you both, but not me, yet. I'll take her out tomorrow. Let's just match the number and name and address, and boom." This was Mitchell's clean-cut pragmatic solution, and it had its merits.

"I have a concern," Hadley said. "Who is she? what does she know? and why is she doing this? As soon as we know that we'll take her out or whatever."

"Waiting is risky," Mitchell objected. "That's what the cops did at the warehouse. If they had pulled the trigger, as they should have, we wouldn't be here."

"We're not going to wait," Hadley replied. "We'll get a fix on her first thing tomorrow morning. If it looks bad, we'll take her in for questioning, as they say in the police. Then if she's guilty, we'll prosecute and pass judgement and then, pardon the expression, execute that judgement." This satisfied Mitchell, and they launched into what-if scenarios.

The assumption was that they would need to bring her in for

questioning, after which it was unlikely that she could be considered innocent. For one thing she would be guilty of knowing about her own abduction. The outline plan was that Jim Duggan would pick up a suitable vehicle anyway. The vehicle would be available for Bob Mitchell to perform any necessary abduction. Jim Duggan would call Bill Hadley the moment the abduction was effected. Bill Hadley would then call and leave a message on her answer phone for Jean Galloway to say he had an investment opportunity and he was glad he had managed to get her as he must have taken her number down wrong. With the call coming through at the time of the abduction, this would be his alibi.

***

"I think we're getting it together," John said to Jenny, as they breakfasted in the kitchen of their apartment. Even as he spoke, Duggan was passing the message to Hadley, twenty miles to the north: she's the wife of a police lieutenant, John Ralphs. Mitchell was given the green light.

"I'm going to give Chris a call as soon as he gets in at nine, and suggest I go over there. What are your movements today?" John asked.

"I guess it's back to work for me, after the excitement. I couldn't do that again. But I still can't believe it's that guy, even though I know it must be. I guess I'll head out about nine thirty. I'm going to walk in today. I need the exercise, even if no one else does." It always amused her that she was virtually the only pedestrian in town outside a radius of forty yards from the shopping malls.

"You know, Jenny, even when we've put our bit together, it still gets us nowhere evidence-wise. They have to do something else: make some mistake; provide some lead; give us some hard evidence; and I don't know what that's going to be, unless they do another bank. That's the last thing I want these trigger-happy bastards to do. It's lethal."

"That's why I say, rather my job then yours," Jenny answered. "You have to take crazy risks, and then you're still out in the cold. Yesterday's interview with Hadley was more than enough for me, much more than enough, never again." She smiled at him. Her understanding of his position was a huge boost to his confidence in this difficult situation. She stood up and busied herself around the apartment. It was not even eight o'clock.

Having arrived at six a.m., Hadley sat in his office, anticipating with eagerness the day ahead. This is my command and control centre, he thought. Today I am free to take control. So far I always had to combine this with the role of field officer. Today I'm George W. Bush sending forces into Afghanistan. I'm the Director of the CIA. He chuckled at the notion, and thought about his *forces,* his *field officers.* Duggan is a sly little devil, he thought, but he's weak. He'll carry out his orders to the letter, because he relies on me. And as for Mitchell, well, he's one of the few guys I know these days who likes to watch cowboy movies. He just loves gunning Red Indians down, and failing them whatever else he can get, and that's it for him. He sees no further than that. Still, he seemed to buy into the damsel in distress bit about Ralphs alias Galloway, so she should survive for the time being in his protective custody. I need to interrogate her, to ensure our plans are tailored to the situation. Again, he thought, this is me: command and control; conducting the whole operation from behind the scenes. I'm smart. Even when things went against us and we were trapped in the warehouse, I managed to get us out. Mitchell would have just blasted his way to an early grave, and Duggan would have panicked himself to the same underground destination. I got them out of there. Once we fix this situation, I'm going for a really big heist. I need a bigger organisation. I need a number two to handle execution while I set strategy. I need operatives in the field. The phone rang. It was eight thirty.

"I've given the vehicle to Mitchell," Duggan said. "He's outside the apartment block on foot."

"Thanks." Hadley clicked the phone off. The instruction was to phone in minimal but regular reports, so that he could track progress.

Jenny left the apartment soon after nine. It was just by chance that John glanced out of the window and saw her step onto the street. A large man emerged from a doorway and fell in behind her. At first it did not strike John, but then he thought there was something odd. He looked again, but they were already around the corner. I am being paranoid, he thought, but what the hell. He opened the door and ran down the steps. He raced along the sidewalk, turned the corner and looked up the street. As far as he could see, no man, no Jenny, and she should be on that street. He ran up the street and saw not a sign, not a soul. He ran back. Around the corner a smallish fellow came out of a telephone booth. John screamed the question: had he seen a woman about thirty. The man looked shocked and pointed around the corner where John had seen her go, and moved away fast from this apparent maniac. John rushed back up to the apartment. A message had just been left on the answer phone. He ignored it and called Ross.

Ross alerted his boss and a message went out instantly to all patrol cars. Ross was sent to pick up John and head straight for Hadley's office, even while an action plan was developed. Within three minutes Ross had picked up John, and with sirens blaring and lights flashing, they made it to Hadley's office, twenty miles to the north, in fourteen minutes. They burst in on Hadley, who was reading a stockbroker's circular, and showed him their ID.

"Gentlemen," Hadley said, perfectly calm and motioning to the two chairs in front of his desk, "do have a seat. What can I do for you?" John and Ross looked at one another. The voice, their looks said, it's uncanny.

"When did you get here?" John started, but looking at the blotter on Hadley's desk, saw his own phone number. "What's this?" he asked, pointing to the number.

"A Mrs Galloway," Hadley responded. "I've just called her

about an investment opportunity. She was in yesterday. A new client. Unfortunately she was out, so I left a message on the answer phone."

"Excuse me," John said. He stepped outside the office and pressed the shortdial for home on his cell phone. When the answer phone came on, he punched in his security code, and sure enough Hadley's voice came on the line, very proper, very courteous, not a trace of tension. For security reasons John had instructed Jenny not to use their name in the answer phone message, so Hadley could fairly claim to believe that he had recognised Jean Galloway's voice and left a message. John went back into the office, but he let Ross complete the routine questions. Outside John said to Ross that Hadley must be in the clear, otherwise he was one hell of a cool customer. They had not expected to see him sitting in his office, let alone making a call to John's number. She wasn't supposed to give him our number, he said to Ross. Why did she do that? Much later it would occur to them that maybe she had not.

Back in the patrol car John turned to Ross.

"They've got to take me off suspension," he said. He reached for the radio.

"This is Ralphs here, I need to speak to the captain."

A few seconds later: "Ralphs?"

"We've drawn a blank up here, Sir. They have my wife. I request to be taken off suspension." John spoke evenly, without showing his emotion.

"Maybe that's why you should stay on suspension, Ralphs."

"No, Sir. If ever my expertise can be of use, let that be now," he persisted.

"Come and see me, Ralphs."

"It's looking good," Ross said, squeezing John's arm.

Jenny had left the apartment in good spirits, happy to have the unpleasant experience of yesterday behind her. As she turned the corner, she sensed a movement behind her. A hand came over her nose and mouth, and she felt the click of a handcuff around the left wrist. She was pulled back a fraction as the man's left hand reached past her and pulled open the car door. She was thrust into the back seat, felt the click of the other cuff on her right wrist and a hood came down over her head. The front door opened and closed. She was lying on her right side, but could not change her position, as the handcuffs were attached to something behind her. Breathing was difficult under the hood. She heard the car start and it moved off, swinging immediately into a road on the left. Side roads, she thought, but very soon lost any sense of direction, and terror set in.

CHAPTER FIVE

Back at the farmhouse they enjoyed lunch in good spirits.

"Gentlemen, may I call you gentlemen?" Hadley joked. "We are good at what we do. We make a good team. Yesterday we sniffed out a nosy female investigator. Today we have a police lieutenant's wife locked in our cellar."

"Are you sure that's safe?" asked Duggan with his usual insecurity.

"Couldn't be better," said Hadley. "The only link to us was made by them and not by us, so they have no reason to come here and certainly no justification for a search. This is the safest place."

"I'll shoot her now," suggested Mitchell.

"I'm not so sure," Hadley replied. "Let's make a plan. You know what. I think this may be a good time to rob a bank, while the police are hunting abducted police wives, you know, otherwise engaged."

"You have a bank in mind?" queried Duggan.

"Funny you should ask." Hadley had a smug grin on his face. "I was thinking about the branch on Main Street. Go for the safe this time."

"You out of your mind?" It was Mitchell's turn to assert himself.

"That's exactly it, Bob," Hadley replied. "Who in their right mind would rob the same bank three times in a row? No one. Right?"

"Right." Both Duggan and Mitchell assented to that.

"So that's settled then," said Hadley. "We will, because they won't expect us to rob it for one moment."

"But I'll shoot the woman first." Mitchell was back on his favourite subject.

"Let's put that on hold for the present," Hadley proposed. "In the back of my mind I have another thought. She doesn't know who we are. If we can think of a way of using her to keep the attention off us and maybe shift attention somewhere else, it could even be interesting to release her. We can shoot someone else, Bob."

"I like that one," Duggan cut in. "Let's explore that. We might need some kind of *get out of jail free* card."

"She's a very attractive woman with a very engaging manner," Hadley continued. "I enjoyed the interview with her yesterday. So remember she is our guest. I want to make it comfortable for her down there. Also, and I know I don't need to say this to you gentlemen, we are not going to rape her or otherwise molest her. On the one hand, we are civilised human beings, and on the other hand, we do not wish to plant any unnecessary forensic evidence. Frankly, we should avoid all physical contact. That's another reason why I want her to have access to the bathroom down there. Let her wash off any evidence that might have resulted from the abduction. We'll get her some fresh clothes and burn those she's wearing."

"I'm still keen to learn what she was after and why," Duggan squeaked, bringing them back to the issue in hand.

The bounce had gone out of Jenny. Her wrists were chaffed from the cuffs, her head ached from the poor air under the hood and her whole body was stiff from the awkward position in the car. As soon as they released her in what appeared to be a basement, she drank what seemed like gallons of water. Agitated she paced the room, and after a few minutes decided she should examine the detail of where she was, in case there was a clue to where she was or who these people were. It had to be Bill Hadley from yesterday. When would John miss her? Would he have Hadley pulled in? She looked around. The room was set up like a guest room with a bed, an armchair and a small wardrobe. There were two doors. The one by which she had entered, which was locked, and next to it a door which led into a shower room with a toilet and washbasin, where she had drunk the water. Ventilation was by way of fans in a narrow shaft. Natural light came in through a section of translucent glass bricks set just below the ceiling. There was no indication as to where she was and no way out other than through the locked door. She saw a telephone point next to the bed, but no telephone. A basket of fruit was on the table as well as a tray with biscuits and packets of fruit juice. Then the thought of their dead friends hit her, and she began to tremble uncontrollably. Sobbing, she crawled into the bed, closed her eyes and wished herself elsewhere, but to no avail. Behind closed eyes one nightmare scene succeeded another, until totally out of control, she was screaming with rage and despair. She must have fallen asleep, because when she finally threw the bedcovers from her, there was a tray of food, placed next to the food basket, with salad, boiled eggs, cold meats, bread and a thermos flask of hot coffee.

I am not playing this right, she thought. I must keep my wits about me and find out what is going on. I must pick up any clues I can, so that when John finds me I can provide valuable information to help catch these men. What are hostages supposed to do? I'm supposed to bond with them, so that they do not harm me. Again she shuddered at the thought of these callous, ruthless men who gunned down innocent people. She lay back and thought of John. She saw his tall frame before her, imagined his eyes flashing with anger when he found she had been kidnapped and trusted herself to his power to rescue her.

John had not been told whether or not he would be reinstated, but no one objected to his presence. Ross had unofficially been assigned to look after him, but confusion reigned in the precinct. There had to be a link between the two robberies and there had to be a link to the kidnapping of Jenny Ralphs. Hadley was the obvious link, but that did not seem to stack up. If anything it was John who was bringing order into this chaos. He moved around, questioning the members of the team, trying to develop thought processes, looking for an angle to follow up. Forensics had turned up nothing to go on so far. John ignored the suggestion that he should be at home waiting by the phone in case a call came. That was too simple, he thought. This is not a straightforward kidnapping. If and when they want to get hold of me, they will. They must know who Jenny is. This is not just a random event.

John came back to Ross's desk.

"You know, I never got round to calling Chris," John said. "Maybe it's even more important now, than it was. We should go ahead with our plan. It might help Jenny."

"I'll call him now." Ross picked up the phone, and Chris answered on the first ring.

"Hi, Chris. You've made a tape? Great. We'll get it now. There's bad news, Chris. John's wife, Jenny. They've got her." The shock on the other end of the line was palpable.

"OK," John said, as Ross hung up, "can we organise this, that everyone who was at the warehouse at the time of the hostage scene gets to listen to the tape and gives us his view? Maybe it's not evidence, but it might confirm whether or not we are aiming in the right direction."

John returned to his apartment late that evening. As he knew it would, the emptiness and the loneliness struck him. In the afternoon he had advised immediate relatives of the situation. Jenny's parents had taken it well. He had asked them not to come over, but to let him get on with the job. It was a harrowing experience. So far friends did not know, and the longer that lasted the better. He did not want interminable expressions of sympathy. In his professional capacity he had requested at Jenny's workplace that they keep quiet about it. Publicity was not felt to be of value at this stage, certainly not before they had developed a better understanding of what was going on. This was all the practical side. With this he could live. But the victim was Jenny this time, not just a victim. Where was she? How was she? What were they doing to her? How was she taking it? His mind went round and round in turmoil. He looked out of the window to where it had taken place. He flicked on the television. He turned it off. He made some coffee, and then poured it away. Restless, he wanted to go out, but he wanted to stay in. He decided to get some sleep, but lay awake with the same thoughts running through his mind over and over. The defence lawyer towered over him: "So this is the man you saw," he said, pointing at Hadley. Ralphs: "No, no, that is the man I heard." Defence lawyer: "The man you heard. Ladies and gentleman of the jury, consider carefully this man is not an eyewitness; he is an earwitness." "No you don't understand…" John awoke with a start. God this is awful, he thought. How can this have happened? Where is she? What can I do? He checked the dial of his watch – four a.m. He decided to get up. I'll try to set pen to paper, and see if that helps with a plan, he thought.

At six John called Ross and invited himself to breakfast to expound his plans.

"The point is, Ross, that we precipitated the kidnapping with our plan to entrap Hadley. Now let's assume Hadley is guilty and playing a very clever game. In that case, we have to be even cleverer."

"Any thoughts as to how, John?"

"Well, we've got to be quick. I really believe that time is not on our side if we are going to get Jenny out. That means we cannot simply investigate. We've got to make something happen."

"Like we've already made something happen," Ross said.

"What we have now, Ross, is the tape. I say we doctor it a bit and add in a bit that sounds like Kinley on the megaphone. Then we have to work out a way of confronting Hadley with the tape, claiming we recorded him at the warehouse. It has to be a plausible confrontation. No doubt he will deny it, but it will prompt him to take action. If he's hasty he might make a mistake."

"Are you not worried about increasing the danger to Jenny?"

Ross countered.

"I am acutely aware of the danger she is in," John said, "and I see that danger growing every day that we do nothing. If Hadley perceives himself to be in danger, surely that will take pressure off Jenny to some extent. Well, that's what I have to hope. I see no other way."

"Then we have to work out a way of confronting Hadley in a way which is constructive," Ross said. "Not that he just cuts and runs."

"Right, Ross. Let me make one thing clear. This is about Jenny. This is also about Kinley and the rest of them. Jenny took this risk for them. I want her out, and I want her risk to be rewarded, her personal risk which she took for our friends, and to stop these bastards ever doing something like this again. That's what this is about, Ross." Determination set upon John Ralph's face.

A thought began to form in Ross's mind. "You know, John, Hadley is not the weak link. You saw how much he was in control, when we were in his office. Confronting him with the tape would be like revealing your hand in poker. I think we should pull in either Duggan or Mitchell. Now Duggan's the other one with a voice that people heard, the shrill voice in the bank – he's the guy who talked in the bank. If we went after Mitchell, we could claim we have Duggan on tape as well. We could claim it's even more damning, but only play Mitchell the Hadley tape."

"You saw Mitchell and Duggan, Ross, when you checked out the alibis. What were they like physically," John asked.

"Duggan's a weedy fellow and Mitchell is a very big man," Ross answered.

"Well you know what. It was a big guy whose back I glimpsed in the street when Jenny was kidnapped. If it was one of these three, then it was Mitchell." John felt a plan was coming together. "What have we got to lose? If it was him, we can rattle him, and if it wasn't, too bad. Let's try to unnerve them, and see where we go from there.

It was not difficult to track down Bob Mitchell, as he worked from home. Mitchell opened the door to John, towering over him as he lead him through to the lounge. John wasted no time. He simply pulled the tape player from his bag, set it on the table and pressed the play switch. Bob Mitchell listened to the tape in silence. Across the table sat John Ralphs. In a car outside listening in on a radio receiver sat Ross, which Mitchell did not know. The tape clicked off.

"We have another tape, one of Jim Duggan in the bank," John said.

"Well, that sure sounds like Bill Hadley," Mitchell admitted.

"Look, Mr Mitchell, I'm not accusing you of anything. I'm asking you to help us." John looked Mitchell square on. He had to persuade this man that there was a way out for him, if they could get to the big fish. "You know these people, and we believe they may be involved in criminal activities. We are appealing to your civic duty."

"I don't see what I can do for you. Yes, I know Bill and I know Jim. I know lots of people." Mitchell replied firmly in his deep voice.

"We're looking for information, Mr Mitchell. If you had any, or knew anyone who could help, well, if it was incriminating for them, we would do a trade, do a deal with them." John felt he was not being very subtle in insinuating that there was a deal for Mitchell to take.

"If what you say is true," Mitchell said, "then I fear for my own safety. More so now that you have asked me to listen to this tape."

"Your own safety?" John queried.

"Yes, think about it. If what you say is true, now I know too much. So what do I do?" Bob Mitchell looked at John questioningly.

"You come in and talk to us," John answered.

"Either that," Mitchell responded, "or I take off. I have no ties here."

"No, think of the threat these people pose. Talk to us," John insisted.

"First comes me, as far as I'm concerned." Mitchell sounded adamant. "But I'll do a deal."

"Tell me the terms." John leapt at this change of heart. The mood was changing in his favour. A vision of Jenny moved to the front of his thoughts.

"The terms? There are no terms. My safety: that's all. Jim's meeting Bill in his office at four. I know because they asked me to come over." Mitchell held John's gaze. "You give me a guarantee and I will talk."

"What's the guarantee?" John asked.

"No, not a guarantee. From what you tell me these guys are too lethal for you to guarantee anything. I'll tell you what. You take these guys in. When you have both of them locked in a cell, I'll talk. You call me here when you have both of them locked in a cell, and I'll drive into town. I'll come and see you. Is that a deal?" On his own John could not have made a deal. With Ross listening in and recording everything outside in the car, he thought there could be a deal. Anyway, it was all he had. Mitchell had made a proposal. The ball was in his court.

"It's a deal," John said.

As John got in the car, Ross gave a low whistle.

"Wow," Ross exclaimed, "that is some deal. What do we do?"

"Ross, you call on the radio while I drive, and you recount my conversation with Mitchell to HQ. Then propose two things. One: they take the surveillance of Hadley's farmhouse and Duggan's bungalow and move everyone pronto to Hadley's office. Two: with as much back up as can be mustered, they hit Hadley's office at four and take them both in for questioning."

Bob Mitchell had watched Ralph's intently to make sure he did not place any bugs while he was there. Now he relaxed. He took a beer from the refrigerator in the kitchen and threw himself down in his television recliner. The bedroom door opened and Bill Hadley stepped out.

"I'm gonna recommend you for an Oscar, Bob." Bill was

smiling broadly. "Do they have one for best actor without a script? That was perfect, sending them to my office."

"I'm not just a pretty face, Bill. My brawn is matched only by my brain. Clearly they've got us pinned down, so I had to send them off somewhere believable," Bob replied.

"I think it's time we went on holiday. Plan B. We'll call Jim at the farmhouse now. The clock's ticking." Bill was already reaching for the phone.

Bill Hadley had honed the planning process to what he considered to be perfection. Each scenario would be set out on paper, graphically displayed so that it was 100% clear to each of them. The likely course of events was set out in a planogram, as he called it. Decision boxes in the planogram led to different courses of action, depending on the decision required by circumstances. Weaknesses and risks were calculated and listed. Hadley's view was that the simplest plan was the best plan and the simplest plan usually entailed risks. Therefore things would go wrong but that did not matter because countermeasures were planned in.

A frequent symbol in the planning process was a red revolver, which meant, *we shoot our way out*. This symbol had been used several times on the decision tree leading from the bank just over three weeks ago. Hadley had learnt that while violence could be counter-productive, extreme, sudden violence was highly effective. Hadley had rented a cabin by a lake for the "holiday" plan. The plan was simple. Wherever they were, they would all head for the cabin. The risk in this case was surveillance and that any one of them might be followed. The initial phase of this plan had a number of red revolvers drawn in on its planogram.

Jenny was sitting in the armchair dreaming of home, of her apartment, of John, when she heard a rustling sound. A typed note had been slipped under the door.

Mrs Ralphs,
It has unfortunately become necessary to bring you to a place of

greater safety. I do not wish to harm you, and I regret the insult to your dignity when I brought you here.

I ask you to co-operate. I am on my own and I do not wish to be obliged to employ force. I respect you, and admire the fortitude you have shown in bearing these regrettable circumstances.

In the draw at the bottom of the wardrobe you will find a black hood. It has holes for your mouth and nose, so that you may breathe freely. Please pull the hood over your head and knot the drawstring below your chin. You will also find handcuffs. Please cuff both wrists in front of you. In ten minutes I will lead you out. Unfortunately, the first part of the journey must be in the trunk, but I assure you that this will be for no more than a few minutes, before we change vehicles. By the way, there is no purpose in trying to get a look of me. I shall be disguised.

Please accept this note for what it is: an attempt to make an unpleasant task as bearable as possible. Take my assurance that this will be over soon.

Panic surfaced and subsided. *This will be over soon,* she thought, and grabbed at that straw. She reached into the draw, carried out the instructions and waited, in her own personal darkness. She heard the lock and then the door. A touch on her shoulder and she was guided up the stairs and along a corridor. It was eerie underneath the hood, pitch black. Another door and they stepped into a room with a hard surface. Then the click of what must be the catch of the trunk, and she was gently helped into the trunk and the lid slammed above her. Her calm up to this moment dissipated and she began to sob, more in self-pity than fear. The note had had a calming effect, clear and courteous, somehow removing the immediate threat. A moment's panic: will I suffocate in here? And then the motor sprang to life and they were moving.

In the driver's seat, Jim turned out into the road with Jenny in the trunk, tapping numbers into his phone. Bill answered from his vehicle.

"No surveillance so far," Jim said.

"OK continue towards the track. Approach slowly until you see us in the distance, and then set your speed so that you turn in immediately behind us. Even if it comes from nowhere out of the bushes, no police vehicle is to get between us," Bill instructed. Bill had given Jim a start time which should result in them arriving together almost to the second, meticulous as ever. The road ahead was a clear stretch of a mile and a half. Jim saw his partners' vehicle approaching. He checked his mirror and still there was no sign of life behind. On the road ahead his partners were the only ones in sight. Up ahead was the track, on Jim's right. Bill's vehicle cut across in front of Jim, and Jim followed it, turning into the track just ten feet to the rear. One hundred yards further, the track entered woodland and curved left. Jim saw Bob roll out of the passenger door on the move and take up position behind a tree, aiming a high-powered rifle back from where they had come. Fifty yards further was a clearing with black pick-up truck. There was a superstructure mounted on the rear of the truck to create a separate cabin with smoked glass windows.

By the time Duggan had transferred Jenny to the rear cabin of the pick-up truck, Bob had sprinted up to join them. The clearing was a start point for hikers and hunters and it was not unusual for vehicles to be left there for a few days. The pick-up pulled off across the clearing and they headed up another track to join a different road. Fifty yards before they reached it, Bob jumped out, recced the road up ahead and waived them on, boarding the pick-up truck as it turned onto the road.

"Boring," Bob said.

"You mean no shooting," Jim squawked. "As far as I'm concerned, no surveillance this time was good news. Let's go fishing."

And Bill hit the gas pedal. In the back Jenny sat on cushions with her left hand chained to the pick-up and her right hand free. The hood was removed, so she could follow the route, although nothing looked familiar to her and she did not know from where they had started. Next to her was a bottle of water, a thermos flask of coffee and a picnic hamper. She was no longer nervous, but too resigned to her fate to think of giving these kidnappers a star rating just yet.

The police had taken up positions outside Hadley's office. John had not been reinstated, at least not yet, but he was allowed to come along, given his central role and that he was technically a victim through his wife. They did not know if Hadley was inside. They would wait for Duggan to show up. Four came and went. Four thirty came and went without Duggan. They decided they would have to send someone in to check out what was going on. They chose a low-key approach with an officer out of uniform who might have been anyone. It took thirty seconds to establish there was no Hadley. Expecting the worst, they had moved everyone over here to provide support in case Hadley resisted arrest. Now they had to check out the three men's residences. That took longer but yielded the same result. What struck John, in particular was that Mitchell was gone, the man who had agreed to speak to them, his great white hope for Jenny's rescue. He looked across at Ross and could not stop the tears forming in his eyes, tears for Jenny, tears for Jenny and for him.

CHAPTER SIX

It took them just over two hours to reach the lakeside cabin. They had hooded Jenny for the final stretch and now Duggan transferred her to a room at the rear of the cabin, with a window looking straight out at tree trunks. As far as she knew, there had been just one kidnapper. He had not spoken and he had been masked when she saw him. While she sat and gazed through the window at the tree, John was weeping for her in Ross's patrol vehicle. She felt deflated, but terror and panic had left her. She felt lonely. There was no human contact, not even with her gaolers.

Hadley, Mitchell and Duggan sat on the porch overlooking the lake, a beer cooler in front of them.

"We've got to exploit this mess to our advantage," Hadley was saying.

"How do you mean, Bill?" Mitchell asked. "I mean, I don't know why we don't shoot her and be done with it."

"No, Bill, it's better for us if we are not on the run. We'll use this to legitimate ourselves." Hadley was thoughtful.

"Doesn't look very likely to me." Duggan was taking Mitchell's side.

"Think about it. This is not police work," Hadley said.

"What do you mean?" Mitchell asked.

"That stuff with the tape, the girl coming to my office," Hadley explained, "that's not what the police do. This guy's on his own."

"So what good does that do us?" Mitchell was getting bored with this.

"Boys, give me three days. I'm going to get to know about this girl and her man. Then I'm going to turn the tables on them. I'm going to have him back off. That's the plan." Hadley had finished. He stood up and went inside.

Hadley started to type a note on his laptop. Win trust with trust, he thought. They think I am the kidnapper. It follows that if they trust the kidnapper, then they will trust me. Because they trust me, when I make it clear that I am not the kidnapper, then they will believe me. If I am not the kidnapper, I am not the bank raider. Therefore they have no reason to investigate me, or Duggan, or Mitchell. Mitchell will say he took off because he was frightened when I was not arrested. He effectively told them that he would do that. The logic may be circular, but it is logic. Earth exists so god must have created it: god must exist or he could not have created earth. What's good enough for the Pope is good enough for me. Win trust with trust. I am going to give her my trust.

Jenny saw the door open three inches. A hand reached in and dropped a sheet of paper and a cell phone. She picked up the paper.

You may talk to your husband for twenty minutes. I suggest you call his cell phone. Do not make any other calls. It will not help and we will withdraw this privilege. If you follow the rules, you can call him tomorrow as well. First, tell him you have twenty minutes, but this is a personal call, not business, and definitely not police business. Tell him there are two rules, just two rules. Rule one is that you do not talk about kidnapping. Rule two is that you do not try to describe where you are (it would be a waste of time anyway, as you have no idea of where you are). Tell him to respect these rules.

We have no desire or intention of harming you or him. Oh, and you can mention that we expect to have you out of here and back home within three days.

Jenny's hand trembled as she reached for the phone. She would not believe this until she heard John's voice on the end of the line. Slowly she tapped the numbers willing the call to go through.

"Hello." It was John's voice. For a moment she could not speak. "Hello, hello." His voice repeated and she had to force herself to speak. As emotion flooded through her it came out in a whisper.

"John."

"Jenny, are you alright. Jenny, where are you?" Panic was rising in his voice. She looked down at the paper, drew herself together and read out the rules.

"Do you understand, John?" she asked. "Do you agree to these rules?" He did, and the tension dissipated as they talked. Normality was returning for them both, but twenty minutes was short. She watched the last minute of those twenty minutes slip by on her watch and then respected the trust given to her. She replaced the phone by the door. A hand reached in and withdrew it.

Hadley went back out onto the porch, where the empty beer cans were building. The late afternoon sun was playing on the water, which lapped against the stony beach. Birds flitted across the lake catching insects as they flew. Behind the cabin rose the leafy backdrop of wooded hills with the buzz of wildlife.

"Nice holiday." Bill brought his arm round in a flourish towards the view of the lake.

"What you been doin' in there?" Bob smiled at him and winked. "Something sweet in there, Bill?"

"My plan is going to work. On day four we release her and go home. Now I'm going to take her for a walk. It's part of the plan."

"You what?" It was Jim.

"Look, if she does anything wrong, I shoot her, OK, and we get out of here," Bill said. This satisfied Bob, who told Jim to pipe down.

There was a rear exit from the cabin, which opened onto a path leading straight into the woods. Jenny stepped through the door and set off along the path. The written instructions were clear.

You have been cooped up too long. Go for a walk. Keep to the rear of the cabin in the woods and be back in thirty minutes. I shall be behind you, well disguised, but still, please, do not look at me. You may exchange greetings with anyone you meet, but not more than that, or you must accept the consequences for them. You must be lonely. Feel free to talk. I will listen, but not reply. It is nice to know someone listens to you when you are lonely.

At first she had not been sure, if she should go, but the trees through her window, the outside, had beckoned. A talk with her husband and now a walk in the woods. She began to hum to herself, and then, as if remembering the last sentence, she began to talk out loud, softly at first, but someone was listening and she gained confidence. She wondered about her friends at the office, and voiced this. Then she moved on to John and how he was coping with this ordeal. Afterwards this would seem surreal to her, but at the time, after days shut away, it seemed so natural. The listener had her entire sympathy for that moment, until suddenly she realised time had slipped away. Forty-five minutes had elapsed. Had she broken a rule? He was following her steps as she walked wistfully back to the cabin and captivity. It is said that a special relationship develops between a torturer and his victim, one of mutual dependency. This was no torture, this was control and a special relationship was developing, but it was one-sided.

As soon as Bill left, Bob turned to Jim and threw him another beer from the cooler.

"Bill's good at planning," Bob said to Jim. "I can't say I like this releasing idea."

"Me neither," Jim agreed.

"I think I'll give Bill some more planning to do," Bob continued.

"Yeah?"

"Day four, in the morning, I shoot her." Now that business was out of the way, Bob turned back to his beer.

On day two Bob suggested to Bill that they take a boat out on the lake and go fishing. Bill decided to stay back and work on his planning scenarios, but Jim joined him. They walked around the lake to a clubhouse where they were able to hire a Dory and pick up some fishing tackle. Neither of them knew how to fish, but what the hell, they were on holiday. First stop was back at the cabin where they picked up a beer cooler and accepted Bill's challenge to haul in some fresh fish for dinner. Out on the lake, the shore was soon distant and the colour of the water faded from the green reflection of the trees into the deep blue of the sky. It was wind still and with gentle ripples giving texture to the surface of the water.

"Bill's getting sweet on her." Bob was gazing back at the cabin, wondering about Bill.

"Bob, Bill doesn't get sweet on anyone. I've known this guy for years. He's what they term a psychopath." Jim was pretty clear in his mind about who Bill was.

"Then we shouldn't let him alone with the woman," Bob responded.

What do you mean? You said you were going to shoot her anyway," Jim countered.

"Exactly." Bob opened another beer. "Do you believe in evolution?"

"You mean like we were apes?" Jim questioned.

"Yeah, you see I think I'm very evolved. Do you want to know why?" Bob asked.

"No, I don't," Jim replied.

"Well, I'll tell you anyway," Bob continued. "I was reading this thing about how Europeans developed this gene giving them tolerance to alcohol, which Native Americans, for example, don't necessarily have. Because the Europeans lived in dirty little towns and villages the water wasn't safe, so they drank alcohol. Natural selection eliminated those who couldn't take it. So drinking alcohol is advanced evolution. There's a gene for it."

"So what's that got to do with you?" Jim wasn't particularly interested, just polite.

"Well, I'm leading the way. According to the current state of medical knowledge someone like me should be dead." Bob grinned. "I'm supposed to drink two beers a day max. Imagine."

"That's beyond my imagination, Bob."

"Exactly. I'm leading mankind in the direction of a world where it can survive on liquor alone. Just think. You could store your next thirty years of nourishment in your basement. You'd never have to work, or in our case rob a bank, again."

"You're a real intellectual, Bob, when you can't find anything to shoot."

"I'm serious about dealing with this woman, Jim. Bill's a clever guy, but I can't have him taking risks with my future. He should have discussed this with us, like we discuss the raids." With that Bob turned his attention to fishing.

Back at the cabin, Bill was toiling away over his laptop. He could see a way to ingratiate himself into the Ralphs' household and exonerate himself. Where he had a problem was how to handle her release: how to do it and how to time it. His mind drifted to her in the back room, and he decided it was time for another walk. He typed up a note for her and slipped it under the door. Five minutes later they left the cabin, following the same procedure as the previous day. Jenny, naturally a bubbling, buoyant person had something of the spring lamb about her as she stepped out into the woods, freed from her stall. He followed, admiring her movements and hoping her spirits would bubble over into speech again today. She knew she had a listener, she felt it, and soon the words were flowing. Bill was building his mental picture of her, her psychology and her relationship with her husband. He was looking for the trigger points he would use to draw them to him. Later everything would be recorded on his laptop for analysis and reference, but for now he was simply alert and attuned to her psyche.

The days of the kidnapping were passing slowly for John. To hear

Jenny had been an immense relief, especially when she had been permitted to call again on the second day. Otherwise, he had nothing to do. He was still suspended. He could think of no way of tracking Jenny, and he cursed himself for having involved her. It had to be that trio, he thought, but somehow all the pieces did not seem to fit. Ross, stretched beyond belief, had little time for him. The fact that the case had gone way beyond the local level, just seemed to generate that much more work for him, answering the investigators' queries and undertaking assignments for them locally. Still there was no progress worth mentioning, and there was an argument about whether Jenny's kidnap was really tied in to the robberies. John felt a kind of resignation settle on him. All he found himself doing was waiting for her next phone call. Outside the twenty minutes with her on the phone, the day was a haze of nothing, and so day three passed. At five a.m. of the fourth day, sleeping fitfully, John woke to the sound of the answer phone in the lounge. He leapt out of bed, but the caller had hung up by the time he reached the machine. The light was flashing. He pressed play and heard an unbelievable message.

It was an hour earlier that Bill Hadley had awoken with a jolt. There was something about Bob Mitchell these last couple of days which eluded him. Now it came to him. Whatever topic was under discussion, Bob always came out with something about shooting, representing, in his book, the approach of the true red-blooded male. For two days he had not talked once about shooting. Did that mean he was hiding something from Bill? Bill guessed it meant Bob was planning to shoot someone, and he did not have to look far to decide who. He had proposed they leave at seven. Now he had to get her out of there fast before Bob executed his plan. He threw off the covers, turned on the laptop and he dressed while it booted up.

Jenny awoke to a light scratching on her door and saw a note slipped underneath. He promised I could leave today, she thought. What is this? In the half-light she moved across the room and retrieved the note. She unfolded it and switched on the bedside light.

Be quiet, be quick, be ready in three minutes. You're leaving. Trust me.

Her heart pumped. She was ready. She had always been ready, dressed at night for a rapid exit, if the chance arose. She waited and those three minutes, dragged and dragged. She looked at her watch. Just one minute elapsed. God, please, please. Two light years later, she heard the click of the lock outside as it was very gently, almost soundlessly released. This did not seem right. As far as she knew, there was just one kidnapper. What was he afraid of? Were the police on their way? Was this a ruse? Should she resist? As she started to speak, he clamped his hand over her mouth and dragged her out towards the woods, the way she had gone on her walks. Under the darkness of the trees, he released her and she shivered with both fear and cold, feeling herself truly at his mercy, and fearing the worst. The trembling spread through her limbs.

He pulled out another note and struck a match so that she could read.

Call your husband and give him the address below. Tell him he may tell no one, come on his own and find you safe and unharmed. Or he may call the police. Then he may come here with or without them and retrieve your corpse. It is his choice. I do not mind either way.

You must hide where I take you now. Do not come out until you hear your husband's voice. Repeat do not under any circumstances come out. He should be here in two hours.

As he led her further into the woods, she keyed in the number. The answer phone came on. John, John, she whispered to herself, answer it, but he did not and she left the message as instructed. She was given no second chance. He took the phone from her and indicated that she should crawl into a clump of thick bushes. He left.

Back at the cabin, Bill went to bed. He was awoken at six by Bob's booming voice.

"She's gone. Where the hell is she?" Bob burst into Bill's room, and Bill leapt out of bed.

"It's OK. I advanced the plan, Bob. It's safer that way." Bill spoke evenly, with a faint smile. Bob had a pistol in his hand and was gesticulating wildly.

"I'm going after her," Bob roared. He flew out of the rear door of the cabin and crashed through the woods. Bill walked out onto the porch, where Jim was munching breakfast.

"I don't think I should go after him, Jim. I think you should. I think you should let him know that it won't be good if she sees him. Right now we have no eyewitnesses." Jim was reluctant to stalk a raging armed Bob Mitchell through the woods, but he saw the point.

Situated just thirty yards from the cabin, Jenny heard the sound of a wild creature crashing through the undergrowth, and was on the point of leaving her hiding place when she realised it was a man. She got a glimpse of an arm waving a gun, but did not see the man. I don't understand this, she thought. First, he hides me and then he's crashing through the woods with a gun. Or is it someone else? But why would anyone be running around with a gun other than the kidnapper? Or is he the police? I should show myself and get this over with. She began to crawl out of the bushes. Then she stopped. The note said wait for John's voice. It was very clear. Surely it's not a trick. She crawled back under cover, just before Jim Duggan ran by in search of the rampant Mitchell.

By the time Mitchell had been retrieved and they had packed up, it was six forty-five. Bill drove the truck off the grass down to the tarmac road and eliminated the tyre tracks. Not that it really mattered. They would abandon the pick-up later. The other two got into the truck, as Bill went back up to the cabin. He set light to the bedding in the bedrooms and the cushions in the lounge, and then he turned on the gas bottle in the kitchen. They drove out past the clubhouse and on to the highway, heading north. Ten minutes later, heading south, John passed a black pick-up truck going in the other direction and thought nothing of it.

In the bushes time was slipping by slowly for Jenny. She realised she had been there for nearly two hours. She just hoped that John had got the message, hoped he would be there, to hear him. That was when she smelt the smoke. At first the faint smell of burning floated in the air, but it grew stronger and soon she could here the crackling of a major fire, and as it caught the smoke belched out. Soon smoke was billowing through the bushes and she began to cough. Where is John? So near and yet so far, she thought. It can't fail now. Please. What's happening? Her panic grew as she choked on the smoke and realised she would not be able to hold out.

As he swung up the driveway towards the lake, John could see smoke rising, and soon he could make out a cabin on the shore, ablaze. His heart sank, as he realised he was too late. Still, he accelerated hard, swerving off the driveway and heading straight over the grass towards the blazing cabin. Stopping just clear of the blaze, he leapt from his vehicle, screaming for Jenny. And then through the smoke, from behind the cabin, he saw a figure moving towards him, now running towards him. She shed tears of relief, as she sobbed in his arms, stricken but saved, and he led her away.

They drove down to the clubhouse, where the emergency had now been recognised, but there was little to be done. John decided it was better to leave, to be on their own, and they headed back the way he had come. He knew he should call Ross with the news, but he could not face it. They were both still in turmoil. She with the knowledge of what she had escaped and he with the knowledge of what might have been. Somehow, they could not talk for the moment, but sat in silence as he drove north. In this last month the whole world had changed.

CHAPTER SEVEN

Driving north with the three of them in the front of the pick-up, Bill Hadley kept a steady banter going with the aim of relieving Bob's morose mood. Eventually he took the bull by the horns.

"You nearly had me there, Bob." He turned towards Bob, grinning. "If you'd shot her, two days of my work on the laptop would have gone out of the window. All my planning. But I woke up at four and suddenly realised I hadn't planned you in right."

"Screw your plans," Bob retorted. "She's at large and I'm at risk."

"Come on, Bob," Bill cajoled him. "You'll get to shoot someone else. Right now I've got it sorted. She's our safely valve. Just sit tight and wait." Bob brightened up a bit. He knew from the past that Bill generally had smart ideas that worked. Well, what was done was done. He could not change it now, and go back and shoot her, so he had better make the best of it.

"Give me another beer, Jim," he ordered, "and think about evolution, right."

As the road ahead came to meet them interminably mile after mile at fifty-five miles per hour, Bill began to think about those walks in the woods. He could feel it was happening again. He knew it would do him no good, but he was drawn to her. It would be just like all the other times, in the end, he knew, when rage would overtake him. Again the thought came to him that he should seek professional help. One of his clients was a psychiatrist locally, very eminent. They were quite good friends. Can he not see it for himself, see into my head, Bill thought? Can he not tell me why this is happening again? Then he rationalised it to himself. No, this time I am completely in control. I can take her or leave her. I do not need help. Bob needs help. Jim needs help. They are both psychotic. You just have to look at them to know that.

In his seat Jim was dozing dreamily. He had half listened to the banter between Bill and Bob, but it did not interest him. How come I get hooked up with these weirdoes? he asked himself. I guess it's the money. Who else has asked me to rob a bank with them? And we do split our shares evenly. Bill plans, Bob shoots and I do whatever they tell me to do. I guess it's OK. When it comes down to it, we do a pretty good job, make a good team. The kind of ultra-violence we use seems to work quite well around here, where the cops prefer to pussyfoot around like ballet dancers. I can't believe they let us just walk out of that warehouse and jump in a fire truck. I guess Bill worked that one out well – when the shit hit the fan, he reversed thrust. Those guys got splattered, well and truly splattered, in all senses of the word. He laughed to himself.

"Well boys, it's been a fun holiday," Bill was saying, as Jim awakened from his reverie.

"Good fishing, if no shooting," Bob added.

"It's back to work tomorrow," Bill continued. "Leave it with me. I'll fix the situation with the cops. Give me three days. Bob, you just tell them you took off scared, if they ask. Just like you said you would, if they didn't call you back. Then say you've spoken to me and you don't believe them. Say it's a load of utter bullshit. The tape must be a fake. It doesn't make sense."

"OK," Bob agreed.

"And Jim, you just tell the cops to go to hell. You're not a nice guy, so don't pretend to be. I think you're a jerk. What do you think, Bob?"

"My mum doesn't like me to use the words that would describe him," Bob replied.

"So your mum told you to wash your hands after you'd been to the bathroom, but that didn't make any difference." Jim wrinkled up his nose, in indication of the source of smell. However, the conversation quickly moved on to professional matters connected with banks and jewellery stores, the latter being an as yet untested business proposition for this little group.

Over the next couple of days the police left the trio in peace. As Ross explained it to John that evening, they were stymied. They quite simply did not know which way to go. Every lead resulted in a dead-end. John had waited to call Ross until they were back at the apartment. He needed to be settled and so did Jenny. She had assured him that she had not been harmed or molested in any way; in fact they had shown her more courtesy than he did. He was about to offer to drive her around in the trunk of the car in the future, handcuffed, but she disappeared into the bathroom with the evident intention of a relaxing morning in the bath. Ross came straight round. They talked the whole thing through, but Jenny had not been able to give John anything on the drive back, other than that there seemed to be just one kidnapper. It had to be connected with Hadley, but then why did he let her go? Why were there no demands? It did not make sense. So maybe it wasn't Hadley. They would have the cabin at the lake, or what was left of it, checked out, but they both knew that that would yield nothing. What next?

"I'm afraid to make another move, Ross." John looked at Ross, pain showing in his face. "We were stuck, so we tried to force them into the open, to make a mistake, and then this awful thing happened, this kidnapping. Then we tried to force the issue again with the tape and Mitchell, and everything went dead. Then I get phone calls from Jenny and she resurfaces. It baffles me. What's it all about? I daren't take another step, for fear of the whole thing spiralling out of control again." Ross sat there and said nothing. He too felt it was beyond him. Finally he spoke.

"They got nothing on the first raid, John. On the second raid they got just under thirty grand. They're going to have to strike again. Let's hope it's not here, but wherever it is we've got to get them. That's all there is to it. There's a debt there, John, a very big debt."

If the financial advisory business had been tedious before, now it was beyond Bill Hadley to focus on it. Most of the time in his office was spent on his laptop, honing his plans. Jewellery was the new project. The raid was easy. What he was working on was a safe way to turn it into cash. What Jim called their ultra-violence was effective on one side of the deal, so why not on the other. If they took a jewellery fence out in a very unpleasant way, then maybe the other receivers of stolen jewels would be more amenable in negotiations. He thought about this and decided he would like to put in place a process. He would start with simple threats, escalate to a bit of minor assault, followed by full-scale torture and execution, with plenty of evidence left behind. They would need some kind of alias, some kind of cover, and he was beginning to think a dirty cop might be the answer. Maybe he could tie two things together, and use as his alias (or more probably Bob's alias in this case), the name of Lieutenant John Ralphs. After all, if things turned really bad, they could always stick a bogus abduction of his wife on him. In fact, the more he thought about it, the better it looked. What it could be made to look like was dirty cop Lieutenant John Ralphs trying, with his devious scheming wife, to frame Bill Hadley, law abiding financial consultant. He smiled and picked up the phone to Jim Duggan.

***

The bell rang at the apartment door. Jenny opened it to see Bill Hadley. Bill Hadley stepped back in surprise.

"Mrs Galloway! I'm here to see John Ralphs. I had no idea you knew him. Is he in? If not, I shall come back later." Jenny was stunned, but did not show it. He was not threatening.

"Do come in," she said. "I'm sure he will be here in a few

minutes. Do wait in the lounge. We're in the kitchen, if you need anything." He might as well believe she was with Mrs Ralphs. It was easier than trying to explain what she had been doing in his office. They moved through into the lounge.

"Jenny, I know it was you." His soft voice surrounded her, but there was no menace. "That's why I'm here. To clear the air. I bear no grudge. I know your husband must do his job. If suspicion has fallen upon me, I must be investigated, as any other citizen." He smiled at her and sat down. She sat across from him. Then the door opened and John came into the apartment. He walked into the lounge and looked at them, baffled. They both rose and Hadley repeated to John his earlier words to Jenny. John motioned for him to sit, taking the centre of the sofa opposite. Jenny was obliged to sit next to Hadley.

"I really wanted to clear the air." His melodious voice continued. "I also felt deeply for Jenny when she was taken away by force. I could not help thinking how brave she must have been when she came to my office, to interview a callous killer, a thief who would stop at nothing. And that is also why I am here." John was embarrassed, not least because his suspicions of Hadley were still there, and now the man was his guest in his lounge.

"I had to do that, Mr Hadley. Our friends died. I had to help find these evil people. I had to help John." Jenny was visibly distressed.

"I accept that." He smiled at John and added, "Someone such as your wife may investigate me any time, Mr Ralphs." Silence fell, and Hadley broke it. "Evil is a medieval word, not appropriate for modern police practice. I would say they are not evil but psycho-pathic."

"What's the difference? Evil is evil." This was clear to Jenny.

"I think there may be a difference, one which is important for police work. Lieutenant Ralphs may agree. A psychopath may be acting in a very rational manner, just with a little less emotion."

"You mean as in gunning down police officers in cold blood," John cut in, willing the discussion to end.

"Consider this. A beautiful woman such as Jenny is kidnapped." He took her hand. "And it pains us." He gently released her hand. "And you, John. You are in love with Jenny. You would risk your life for her. Is that rational? I would feel the same, John, but in this case she is not my Jenny. But if she were and if she loved me, then I too would be ruled by emotion like you, in this particular case. The psychopath experiences less emotion, John. That is all. He wants money. Someone is in his way. He shoots him. This is what mankind does anyway, John, in wars. It is what the psychopath is prepared to do within his own community, and this is what we object to." The words washed around Jenny and she sank back in the sofa next to him. He wanted to draw this out as long as he could as he sat there with her. She could see John as if he were on a distant shore willing her to come back to him, and then the spell was broken. Hadley stood, reluctantly, to leave. He had achieved the first step of what he termed reconciliation, but not as well as he had hoped.

"He's slimy," John said.

"He's not slimy, John. He's a ladies' man. That's why he makes you uncomfortable. His soft voice makes us feel warm inside. He is appealing to us, rather than speaking to us. I felt the same in his office."

"That stuff about psychopaths was weird." John did not want to hear about Hadley's charms.

"It was weird. I'm seeing my counsellor tomorrow." A psychiatrist had been assigned to help Jenny over her ordeal. "I'd like to ask him about this."

"I'll come with you, Jenny. I have my own questions."

Giles Marshall was in his mid fifties, and had practised psychiatry in both hospitals and private practice. As his profession demanded, he had a good listening manner. He had a sleepy look with drooping eyelids that set his patients at ease. He greying hair and lined face added a fatherly impression. He saw little point in seeing Jenny. It was a duty for him and for her. Clearly she was totally together and had no adverse effects from the kidnapping, but they would both go through the motions of counselling as was expected of them. However, he livened up when they addressed the question of psychopaths.

"This is my special draw," he said, opening a locked steel cabinet. Mostly people display a mix of symptoms that make up their particular case. But every now and then I have a patient who brings together all the fragments of the condition in one case, like a full house in poker. These cases I collect for reference. This man – let's call him Al Capone – mirrors what you have just been describing to me." He pulled a file out of the draw of the cabinet.

"Giles, let's do a role-play here," John proposed. "Let's assume that the man we mentioned who told us about the psychopaths yesterday is a psychopath. Describe the situation to us. We'll sit back and listen to your lecture."

"John, Jenny, your man was right. We do now believe that part of the brain is physically smaller in subjects with psychopathic conditions. I won't be technical, so think of it as the seat of the emotions that is undeveloped in a classical psychopath. Your man will appear normal, because in most senses he is normal. If he is highly intelligent, his very rationality may be heightened and dangerous. Because he does not live in our emotional world, at least not in the sense of the rest of us, he may devote considerable energy to planning things that we would never even consider doing. He may establish an objective and then eliminate what stands between him and his objective remorselessly."

"So he's a rational man then?" Jenny asked.

"Don't think of if like that," Giles continued. "He will have desires like you or I, but he will do things to satisfy those desires that we cannot do. He may fall in love, but there he will be thwarted. He may have a well-honed social veneer, but underneath his veneer the person he hopes to love, the object of his affections, will eventually encounter ice, cold steel, call it what you will. In most things he can take what he wants. In love he cannot: it must be reciprocated. This is one classic situation in which he gets dangerous. He may be good looking with exceptional social graces on the surface, which he has learnt, but his emotionally retarded nature will always come through. He may have been rejected many times in the past, and may or may not have controlled his violent reaction, but ultimately it will out, as they say. "

"So if we encountered such a person, what should we do?" John asked.

"What I would do," Giles turned very serious, "is pack my bags and start again elsewhere, if my ties here were not too strong. Speaking as a psychiatrist, I do not believe a healthy man or woman can escape from a determined psychopath of the type you describe."

"Can't he be arrested and imprisoned?" Jenny asked.

"Jenny, he is a very hard man to catch. He is devious, manipulative and very, very aware of what he is doing. He will take care of the last little detail if he is like the man in my file." Giles waved the file and looked very unhappy. John also felt unnerved. He knew what Giles meant. He knew how difficult it was to collect evidence that would stand up in court. The rule of law did not make it easy to catch psychopathic killers, and psychopathic killers seemed the best way to describe the men who had so recently come among them. But who were they?

Jenny persisted: "Can we oblige someone to take a psychiatric assessment, or even get them to volunteer."

"It's very difficult, Jenny," Giles responded. "It's like when you have an intermittent fault in a mechanical device. It's like your washing machine works fine when the repairman arrives, and then cuts out again as soon as he's gone. The human mind is very complex, and this man may be very clever." With this the discussion reached a close. What Giles was unaware of was that John and Jenny were thinking of Bill Hadley, and what John and Jenny were unaware of was that Bill Hadley had been Giles' financial advisor for the last three years, and he and Bill would often meet for a friendly drink, but then it was a small town, and Giles had said psychopaths were hard to spot.

For the coming Saturday John decided to hold a party to celebrate the return of the rescued hostage. Somehow it seemed right to keep it an intimate event with the people who had been involved. The first to arrive were Ross and his wife Mary. In her early thirties, Mary was in the throes of recent motherhood with a son of two and a daughter of eight months, both of whom, after due admiration, would be settled in the bedroom to sleep, or not as the case may be. Still bright and youthful, recent months had wrought lines of tiredness beneath Mary's eyes. Otherwise with her trim figure and shoulder-length blonde hair she could have been Jenny's sister. Next came John's bother Chris with his wife Liz. The women knew one another and John was introduced to Liz, a lively petite lady in her late twenties. Giles might have seemed out of place in this crowd, when he arrived, and maybe his wife Diane, his second wife, was in her way. Diane was a classic older man's wife, these days in the upper echelons termed trophy wife. As she came into the lounge, she could as well have been modelling her green velvet evening gown on the catwalk. Elegant, sparkling, she introduced herself to the gathering, and underneath her exterior she revealed a true interest in each of them. The psychiatrist had chosen wisely after all.

John drew the chairs into a circle in the lounge, and they took their places while he served drinks. As the minutes dragged into double digits, the conversation remained strained. Eventually Jenny decided she had to do something.

"You know, kids, it's like we're teenagers invited to a disco, waiting for the parents to leave, so that we can get going." A laugh went around the circle, nervous not hearty. "There's a subject we're avoiding."

"I can't guess what," Chris chipped in. This time the laugh was less artificial.

"Giles, you take the chair. Let's get it out in the open," Jenny proposed. Giles stood up and moved out of the circle, so that they all had to turn to look at him.

"So what's the agenda," he opened, smiling in his relaxed fashion. "What's the common theme?"

"Abduction?" John suggested.

"So how many of us have been abducted?" Giles asked.

"Chasing the voice," Chris proposed enthusiastically. He had been excited by his success, and in the back of his mind was planning to find a commercial application for this software. His sparks ignited the surrounding timber. This was exactly what they wanted to do: make progress on the case that blighted their town.

"Give me a few moments to think about this," Giles instructed them. "Talk among yourselves." He moved to the kitchen. Immediately the conversation in the lounge developed the buzz that had been so lacking. In the kitchen Giles considered his options. There were a lot of emotions riding on this, probably a hell of a lot more than people realised. He did not want to end up with a catastrophic scene in the lounge. In the end he decided to take an academic approach, to treat it like a sort of seminar and see what came out. He went back into the lounge.

"OK, class, pay attention." Giles struck his professor's pose, waiting for the noise to subside.

"John, tell me what is this, this *chasing the voice?*" He asked.

"Well." John thought for a moment. "It's all we've got, the sound of this guy's voice. We thought if we chase the voice, we'll find him. That's how we got in this mess and…"

"Stop right there," Giles interrupted. He was going to keep tight control of this. "I'm beginning to see the makings of an intriguing proposition. Much research has gone into the voice with regard to lie detectors and so on; much research has dealt with clues to an individuals background and education sculpting the way we speak, but that's more language than voice. We're looking at something different."

Ross: "So what are we looking at?"

"Let's find out," Giles proposed, looking around the circle.

"I'm going to ask each of you what you see in a voice. Chris, you start."

"A voice. Well I deal with a lot of voices, disembodied voices, I suppose, where all I've got is the voice. At work I meet people on the telephone and often only get to see them much later. I used to visualise the person from his voice. Now I deliberately keep it blank. That's really since I met this one guy I'd been dealing with for a couple of years. I went to meet a fifty year old, balding with a paunch and smoking a pipe. In fact, I met this twenty-two year old six foot six athlete."

Giles laughed. "I like that, Chris. You got the message." Giles looked at Jenny. " Jenny?"

"For me a voice tells me of an emotional state. A voice can really move you, like your favourite singer, when you feel a shiver going down your spine, or it can leave you cold, even disgust you, but mostly it affects you one way or another." Jenny would have continued but Giles pointed at Ross.

"I guess it's my work, but I look for what the person behind the voice is thinking and what clues the voice gives me. Is he telling the truth? Is he nervous? I guess I'm a human lie detector." That was Ross's contribution and it moved to Chris's wife Liz.

"I'm probably the reverse of what Chris said. As soon as someone opens their mouth I place them in various categories. Where do they come from, town or country? Did they go to college and so on?" Chris was going to say something but Giles stopped him and moved to John.

"Right now I'm just fixated on that one voice. I hear his words echoing in my ears. I want to nail the bastard." John looked very grim.

"Hmm. I'm not sure you've quite entered the spirit of this little seminar, John, but no matter. As chairman of this convention, I now invite the last participant's contribution, my darling wife Diane.

"Giles, I know this is a trick and that you plan to hold me hostage with your psychiatric horse-play, whatever I answer." She grinned at the others. "But even with your fancy education, when it comes to practical psychology you're no match for a woman. Ladies, you can see who wears the trousers in our household. Voices. There are two types of voice: voices I know, friends and family; and then there are the rest. That's it, Giles. Do with it what you will, but you're not getting me on your couch." She finished to a round of applause. Looking at her, Jenny saw a toughness underneath the veneer of fashion model or society hostess. One tough lady: she could be a marine in another life, Jenny thought, smiling.

"Gentlemen" - Giles took back the reins - "and ladies, if you are still interested, I shall sum up." Mary came out of the bedroom where she had been quieting the kids. "Mary, motherhood excuses you of making a fool of yourself, like the rest of them, but you're in time to hear the results."

"Thank you, Giles." She took a seat.

"Now then, Liz, I'm excluding your contribution. You were talking about language, not voice, which you use to size people up; very valuable but not our subject today. John, I'm excluding you for the reason you gave yourself, you just want to nail the bastard. Are we all agreed?"

"Get on with it, Giles," said Diane.

"That leaves us with Chris, Jenny, Ross and Diane, four differing positions. Let's look at them. Ross, you are the lie detector. You are dealing with how the voice betrays us, with a tremble, a tension, whatever. Interesting and well studied. Agreed?"

"That's it, doc," Ross assented.

"Now, Jenny, I'm going to deal with you and Chris together. Chris had worked out that the sound of a voice does not tell you a person's physical characteristics, including even age. You, however, believe it communicates to you at an emotional level. Tell me, in view of what Chris said, do you really think that the emotion conveyed to you by the singer is shared by the singer? Or is it just a professional performance, just an illusion of emotion?"

"You mean I'm being duped?" Jenny asked. "Duped into believing in an emotion which isn't there. No, I don't agree with you. I think the performer is a performer because she feels and can display emotion, and that's the message I get."

"I agree with you, Jenny." Giles looked at Chris. "So I put it to you, Chris, that you have missed something. You have trained yourself to ignore clues from a voice, false clues, to physical appearance. But you do impute other things, Chris, personality and character."

"Yeah, I sure do that, Giles."

"OK, so what have we got?" Giles started his summing up. "Sorry, Diane, of course, family and friends. What is this? Social cohesion? Familiarity? Like the song we grow to like because we are used to it, or the sound of our mother, soothing us as a child. Diane, I have to think about that. Anyway, what we have is that a voice is distinct from the appearance of a person but it's bound up with things like personality, emotion and mental state, trust, truthfulness, and no one even told me that it speaks words so that we can communicate." Giles stopped here and looked around.

"And John, I wrongly excluded you. What you told us, somewhat abstrusely, is that a voice is unique."

"This is the heart of it, Giles. I have the voice, and Ross and I think we have the man, because he has that voice. But then we find it's not the man." John was agitated.

"Yes, that's it," Ross agreed. "How is this possible?"

"Well, I guess that concludes the seminar," Giles said. "Now it's down to police work."

Diane stood up.

"What a wonderful opportunity you have given me, Giles, to make a fool of you."

"What do you mean?" Giles could see from her sly smile that she had a party-piece lined up.

"Ladies, our men folk never listen to us - well, maybe because we never shut up - here we have an eminent psychiatrist working on a police problem. His wife, me, gives him the very clue he needs, but he's so tied up in his psychiatry that he can't see it."

"My husband's a policeman and he can't see it either," interjected Mary.

"He's a man too, Mary. You've said it, Giles: family and friends. Every voice is unique, but when do we get confused? We call our friends on the phone. One day, in adolescence, the son's voice breaks. We think we're talking to the father when the son answers the phone. It's uncanny."

There was uproar in this little group as the realisation struck home, the false realisation, that Hadley might not be "the voice" but a very close relative of it. Later, much later, Diane would wish she had never made that point.

After the guests left, as she cleared up, Jenny kept thinking, we're just one step away, just one step. I've come so far; I must make it all worthwhile.

Sunday was uneventful, but Jenny was keyed up with anticipation. She left early on Monday morning without even waking John. Bill Hadley was surprised, very surprised, to see her walk into his office and very pleased. He closed the file on his computer, headed "Alias John Ralphs" and stood up to greet her courteously.

"I really wanted to thank you, Mr Hadley, for the consideration you showed, in coming round to see my husband and me."

"I felt it was right, that some way I was implicated in this whole thing." She already felt the warmth of his concern enveloping her. They sat in silence, as she groped for ways of broaching the question that was burning within her, and then it simply came out.

"Mr Hadley, do you have a brother?" His relaxed expression was unchanged, but his mind raced. He could see no reason for the question, but another opportunity to lay confusion opened up to him, and he improvised. A sadness came into his eyes, as he spoke.

"I didn't know I had a brother until my mother died last year." It was true she had died. "Well, just before she died. My father died years ago."

"I'm sorry," she said. In fact, he had not seen his mother for more than twenty years.

"That's OK. She told me she had a child when she was still under age. Same father. It was adopted. When they married years later, it was too late, and then they had me." His sad expression brightened, and another idea came to him. "He lived locally, my brother. She knew who he was. Bad type, she said. Off the rails. I never knew who he was. Found nothing in her papers." He changed the subject. "And you? You've really perked up." It was true. This new information had given Jenny a rush of excitement. So they were on target with "the voice" but it was the brother. Hadley continued on a different tack, and Jenny slipped into the embrace of his gentle tones. It was he who drew the conversation to a close, claiming to have an appointment. As Jenny left, he knew that he did not really understand what was behind her visit, but he was sure that he had taken a major step forward with the tale he had made up about his non-existent brother. He would call Bob Mitchell and they would set the next stage of the plan in motion.

Ross stepped into the Captain's office, a very grave Captain this morning.

"Take a seat, Ross. I didn't want to show you this, but I'm going to." He passed across an envelope, addressed in typeface to the Captain. Ross pulled out a single folded sheet of paper inside the envelope. The first thing he saw was the word "anonymous", at the bottom where the signature should be. He read it. It was short. He looked at his boss.

"I can't believe it's him," Ross stuttered.

"I neither. Tell no one. Watch him. Frankly, I'm not going to do my duty, and you can witness this." He tore up the letter and threw it in the waste bin. "Just you and I know, and that's enough. I don't want those bastards from outside meddling." The Captain signalled that the meeting was over. Back at his desk Ross slumped in his seat and covered his face with his hands. He saw the words of accusation as if the letter were still before him.

Sir,
You might call me a thief but I am not a killer. I will not give you names for fear of my own safety, but there is one among you. My friends, no longer my friends since that disastrous raid, were helped by one of yours, and helped to escape, even when they had murdered his own. I despise him. Do your job.
Anonymous.

It was John who stopped him from shooting them at the warehouse when they boarded the fire truck. John carried on investigating while he was on suspension. Was he trying to allay suspicion? John pushed the whole voice thing and fingered Bill Hadley, even though there was clearly nothing usable as evidence. To divert attention? It was John who reported Jenny abducted and who then recovered her safe and sound. Was this staged? None of it had made sense, but as soon as you slotted John in as the bad guy, then the whole pattern fell into place. Was John playing the assiduous policeman and diverting attention from himself? Even going as far as staging the abduction of Jenny? This is impossible, Ross thought. I have known this man for years. We are best friends. It cannot be. But when I ignore my personal relationship, when I act dispassionately as a police officer, then he looks guilty as hell. It even looks as if Jenny is in it with him. Is there really something I don't know about them?

It was just an hour later that John came with Jenny to see Ross. He met them in a meeting room. John entered beaming. At first he had been angry when Jenny returned from Hadley's office, but this was soon replaced by euphoria, once he realised they were probably right about the voice after all. It was just that they had the wrong brother. Ross listened to them and asked questions, but to John Ross seemed incredibly distant, as if untouched by this momentous news. We just have to find the brother, John was telling him, and better than that he's local, and he's known to be a hoodlum, at least according to Hadley. For his part, Ross's mind was flooded with doubt. *I don't believe this,* he told himself. *He really is incriminating himself. Does he really expect me to believe that he would put Jenny through this after what happened to her last time. It's simply not credible.* Then standing to leave, John said, throwing Ross into total turmoil, "We have to thank, Jenny. If she had told me she was going to do this, there's no way I would have let her. Not after what happened last time."

Twenty miles to the north, Bill Hadley clicked off his laptop, ending the slide show he had projected on the wall for Bill Mitchell.

"So that's it, Bill. You're John Ralphs for this little trip. You won't tell them that, but I'll make sure they find out." They both laughed, Bob with a deep guttural booming.

"Bill, I've always wanted to be a cop. They expect me?"

"I've made an appointment Bob. They want jewels. You have access to them. It's just that when it comes to the negotiation you're gonna threaten the hell out of them. Frankly, I think you're a pretty nasty piece of work anyway, so you should have no problem with that."

"I appreciate your confidence in me, Bill, but I'll keep my opinion of you to myself. Well, not quite. Jim knows it." Bob's whole body rocked with laughter at his own joke, at least he thought it was a joke. "But I'd like to modify your plan, Bill. I think it will have more impact, if I go back to the bar the same night, and, if the guy's in there, break his fingers in front of witnesses." Bill thought about this, and then amended his planogram.

"OK, Bob. I buy that. You're on." With that, the new John Ralphs set out for his rendezvous to negotiate the sale of still-to-be-stolen jewels. Things were looking up. Bob was even beginning to think it might have been right, after all, not to shoot the girl. Bill was one smart dude.

If Bob had seen Bill's planogram, he would have seen a box with him in it, performing a minor crippling exercise on a small-time jewellery fence. He would have seen that this box led to multiple options, to cover what needed to be done next. The problem with using operatives like Bob Mitchell was that you never really knew what they would end up doing in the heat of action. On the other hand, the reason Bill liked to work with Bob was that however of-the-wall Bob's actions may be, he would never end up exposing himself and would always spot a (usually violent) way out of a difficult situation. Bill recognised that, while his own solution had undoubtedly been better, Bob would have found a way to get out, in his own style, when they had been trapped in the warehouse. The unpredictability made it fun.

CHAPTER EIGHT

They were a good hundred miles away from home, which made Bob Mitchell uncomfortable. It was a long way to get back after the raid, particularly if it ended up in a shoot-out, and they were not on home territory. This meant they might have to explain what they were doing there, if anything went wrong and if they were stopped. The jeweller's shop belonged to the man whose fingers Bob had broken in the bar three days before. Wincing with pain, he had threatened Bob with retribution, and Bob, for all in the bar to hear, had said: "Little guy, I'm takin' your shop out. Next time, no tricks with me." The idea behind Bill's plan was to broadcast a message that they were serious and wanted serious prices for their merchandise. *Pour encourager les autres*, Bill had said, and Bob didn't know what the hell he was on about. Still, here he was, and the plan was first to inflict maximum damage, and then steal what they could of value, in that order. If the owner turned up himself, and Bob thought he would, then Bob would shoot him, in the legs this time.

Bob cruised to a stop fifty yards from the store. Ahead, just beyond the store, he saw Jim Duggan get out of his vehicle, that is to say his stolen vehicle, and saunter across to a drug store. He was to be lookout today. Bill was already in the store, posing as a customer. Bob was beginning to feel good. This looks like fun, he thought. Let's get in there. Let's get going. He felt the adrenalin surge that he remembered from his younger days in the football team. He fingered the revolver in his left jacket pocket and then the automatic pushed down the back of his jeans and felt the thrill of impending action. He stepped out of his vehicle and looked up and down the street - calm, peaceful, not a sign to cause concern. He crossed the road and moved down the sidewalk towards the store, listening to the sounds of the street, alert to anything unusual. The traffic was sparse at lunchtime. There were a few young girls out to shop in their lunch break; otherwise, it was sleepy, small town sleepy. Whistling softly to himself as he walked, Bob thought, they need a bit more action around here. Let's hot things up a bit, inject some Latin American rhythm maybe.

Bill was a fussy shopper, or so it seemed to the assistant, who had brought out for inspection one tray of rings after another, followed by necklaces and then earrings. Then Bill complained that she was rude and asked for the manager. As Bob entered the store a furious row was raging between Bill and the store manager. Bob extracted the assistant and told her that if he was to shop in this place, she had better get the owner, and now. She needed little incentive to get away. The owner came down the stairs with the assistant close behind, heading straight for the disturbance that could kill his lunchtime trade. Then he saw Bob, and his good hand moved inadvertently to his bandaged broken fingers, but by this time Bob had slipped round between him and the stairway, and Bill had moved across to the door from the street and released the bolt to lock it. If there were an alarm button, none of the staff, as a result of the dispute, were in reach of it. Right on cue Jim Duggan pasted a "closed" sign on the glass entry door from the outside and moved back to his lookout position. No one moved. No one dared move. The raiders kept silent. They were in no hurry and happy to let tension build. Silence.

Slowly Bill reached for the trays of jewellery. One by one, he took the items out of the display and dropped them into his shoulder bag. Silence. He moved to the open displays and repeated the process. Silence. Wordlessly, he signalled to the owner to have the manager unlock the other displays and cabinets. Unhurriedly, he picked up items, examined them and dropped them into his bag, one by one. Bob reached across to the phone behind the counter. Very deliberately he tapped in Jim Duggan's number.

"All OK outside...Thank you." He hung up. Silence. Bill continued with his examination and appropriation of the jewellery. Time stood still. Silence. Except that every five minutes Bob repeated his phone call to Jim.

Finally, Bill zipped his bag shut and turned to the owner.

"How much do I owe you?" Silence.

"I enquired of you, how much I owe you for these jewels I have selected." Bill spoke in a firm tone. Bob was not surprised by the silence, but it did strike him that nothing had happened other than Bill selecting jewellery and his walking into the store and asking for the owner, (apart from Jim sticking on the closed sign). He thought he should join in the discussion.

"Excuse me, Sir. I believe you are the owner of this store." Bob spoke with the utmost courtesy. "I assume you are the owner, Sir, because the gentleman asked the girl to get the owner and she brought you. Are you the owner, Sir? If so, would you allow this gentleman to pay?" The owner found himself in an extremely awkward situation. He watched Bob's left hand slip into his jacket pocket. He looked at the manager. He looked at the assistant. He turned back to Bill.

"It's on account," he said. "For this volume of purchase you can take your time to pay."

"What's your rate of interest?" Bill asked. There was a sense of menace in the store. The assistant shuddered. Bill thought, in a detached sort of way, I wonder whether Bob will appreciate the changed scenario. We came in here to cause maximum distress and expected little value for ourselves. Now we have a huge amount of jewellery and have no need to shoot and maim these people. Will Bob just shoot anyway, because that is what he does? As it stands, we can sell the whole lot straight back to this bent jeweller, who will have claimed on his insurance by then. He realises this, which is why he is offering to give this to me on "account", hoping I understand the double meaning. What will Bob do?

"I came in here to look for something for my wife," Bob said. "If you remember we met in the bar the other night." He grinned and the jeweller clasped his bandaged hand. "Now it seems that this gentleman has cleaned you out. It's unlikely I will find what my wife wants. But I'll tell you what. I'll go now, but you just take a good look through your storeroom and see if you have any exceptional items. I'll be back in half an hour to see what you've got, if I'm not otherwise engaged. After half an hour, I repeat half an hour, why don't you just go and do whatever it is that jewellery shops do in circumstances like these, you know, when they've been cleaned out of merchandise." Bob turned to the door, unlocked it and left. Bill followed. They left town in the vehicle Jim had "borrowed" for the occasion. With each operation Bill was becoming more impressed with Bob Mitchell's savvy approach and ability to think on his feet, despite the gun-slinging image he favoured.

"One heavy bag. One hell of a load of jewellery. We're rich." Jim Duggan was sitting on the rear seat, examining the contents of Bill's bag. He slipped an Omega watch onto his wrist and liked the look, all five grand of it.

"Bob, call him tonight," Bill instructed. "Tell him to get his abacus out and work out a price for us."

"It has to be a no-brainer for this guy. He knows what his stock's worth, insured for." Bob answered.

"Yeah, tell him to put the price into a couple of lines in the personal section of the Herald and Courier," Bill suggested. "Give him a code word."

"I'll tell him to put it under *broken finger*." Bob roared with laughter. "But why the Herald?"

"It's local to us. The scent trail leads to our town," Bill replied.

"You crazy!" Jim piped up from the bank with a porcine squeal.

"It won't lead to us." Bill glanced behind at Jim and turned back to his driving.

"Well, who?"

"John Ralphs, Jim, John Ralphs." As Bill spoke, a soft whistle escaped from Bob's lips. He was beginning to understand where this was leading and it looked very, very smart. Bill turned off onto a track to make the switch to their own vehicle that was parked there.

Turning into his driveway, Bill saw a patrol car outside the farmhouse, waiting. It was too late to stop and definitely not the place for a shoot out, from his own car at his own house, so he drove up and parked behind the vehicle. At least it was blocked in. An officer got out of the patrol car. Bill remembered him as the officer who had come to his office with John Ralphs. On his side, Ross could see no one through the smoked glass windows of Bill's truck, a Yukon. Then he saw Bill get out and asked if he might have a few words, just routine stuff. Only then did Ross realise that Hadley had not been alone. Hadley turned to the truck, gave a friendly waive and it reversed and pulled off along the driveway back to the road. Ross made a mental note that Bill had been driving and someone else must have slipped across into the driver's seat. It was just his way to remember detail, just in case.

Hadley offered Ross a seat in the lounge and sat down opposite, expectantly.

"We met at your office some time back, Mr Hadley."

"Yes, I recall that."

"We'd like your help, Mr Hadley."

"By all means."

"We are trying to get hold of your brother. To save time, I thought I'd ask you." Ross looked across at Hadley, who looked perplexed.

"I really don't know how you know about my brother. Even I didn't until last year."

"Just his address will do," Ross said in a matter-of-fact tone.

"Officer, I don't even know his name. I've never seen him to my knowledge. All I know is what my mother told me before she died." Bill maintained his air of perplexity.

"But you went though her papers?" Ross raised his eyebrows.

"Nothing. You know what I think. I think this was a hushed up family scandal. Knowing the kind of man my grandpa was, it wouldn't surprise me if they even had the child recorded as someone else's. No way would he have stood for the faintest whiff of scandal. He was a judge. Wouldn't tolerate wrongdoing by anyone, except himself, of course."

"So you mean, he could be anyone?" Ross asked.

"Same father and mother as me, but she said he took after him and me after her. Best I can do is give you a picture of my father," Bill offered. Ross grunted and Bill continued, "There's a chance he doesn't even know he was adopted. Certainly, he never looked for his mother. She saw him locally. Said he was a hoodlum." Bill enjoyed ramming home this tissue of fabrication. I should have been a scriptwriter for soaps, he thought. Ross felt the ground sinking beneath his feet. Bill broke the silence.

"Look. I'll give you a photo of my father, same age as my brother would be today. Stick it in the Herald and ask people to identify him." As he spoke, Bill realised that if they did this, this was how he would specifically link the name of John Ralphs with the raids. Ralphs didn't look anything like Bill's father, but Mr Anonymous would still write in and claim they were one and the same. That would create confusion. Ross registered Bill's smile, which seemed out of place to him.

"I'll take you up on that, Mr Hadley, and we'll see what we do." And they did take up Hadley's suggestion.

CHAPTER NINE

Once again in the Captain's office Ross experienced *déjà vu* as the Captain handed across an envelope. Ross fished out the contents, a sheet of paper, and read it.

Sir,
The man in the photograph? Ask Lieutenant John Ralphs.
Anonymous.

"That's ridiculous," Ross exclaimed. "It doesn't look a bit like John Ralphs.

"I don't think that's what he means, Ross, or she. John Ralphs knows this guy."

"So if this is the guy with the voice, why did Ralphs have to track down Hadley?" Ross was confused.

"I think that's it, Ross. He didn't have to track down Hadley. He knew about Hadley. I always thought that telephone thing worked too well, too smoothly."

"If this is true, it's a disaster." Ross slumped in his chair.

"It's worse than a disaster. Worse, because we have no proof, no evidence." The Captain watched Ross battle with the conundrum.

"There's something more, Ross. A jewellery store was raided a few days ago." He pushed a report of the raid across to Ross. "The rumour circulating over there is that one of our officers is involved. No name yet, but the story goes that it's one of us."

"This is bad." Then Ross summed up the situation: "We get an anonymous letter implying we have a rotten egg; we have an officer on suspension; we get a letter linking that officer to a suspected hoodlum, to use Hadley's word; then rumour connects an officer to a raid, and guess who's got free time right now. And worst of all, the whole pattern of weird events with the kidnapping and everything falls into place if John's the bad guy. He's my best friend, Sir. It was our friends who died."

"As I said, Ross, the worst is we have nothing, nothing, nothing. Everything you said is unsubstantiated hypothesis."

"So we just keep our eyes open?"

"We just keep our eyes open, Ross. You and me." The second anonymous letter followed the trajectory of the first into the waste bin.

***

Feeling trapped in the apartment during the week, John had decided to take Jenny hiking in the hills for the weekend. At first, as they set off through woodland, it had reminded her of the walks in the woods by the lake, but that quickly passed – there she just had someone to listen to her, behind her; here there was communication, two way.

Now they were following the bed of a rocky stream, winding up through the trees. John led the way, on his back a pack with a sleeping bag, food, bourbon and a water filter. He had taken a view on the weather and they were travelling light. They were in a dry spell and it was too early in the year for summer storms. They would sleep under the stars. Dressed in faded jeans and a white shirt, he wove his way among the rocks, crossing from side to side of the stream as the banks steepened, worn away by the springtime run-off. The bare earth was a deep brown behind the grey rocks. The air was filled with the scent of flowering bushes that clung higher up above them to the slopes rising from the bed of the stream. Through the dark trunks of the trees you could see a clear blue sky. They had been walking for two hours. John wanted to reach the point higher up where the trees thinned out to permit distant views, before they stopped for a break. They continued the climb. Jenny felt so good, climbing up through the trees. This was real life at last after the tension of the past weeks, after the drain on her emotions. That was all behind them, and as soon as John's suspension ended, which she knew must be imminent, everything would be back to normal. John wasn't even thinking. He was immersed in nature, with the physical exertion and the joy of the surroundings. His anger was dispersed; the burden was lifted; until they returned it was just Jenny with him and the hills.

They sat leaning against a rock face. Before them they could see the woods dropping away to the plain far below, stretching miles to a distant horizon, where the rim of land curved against the clear blue of the sky. An eagle hung high in the air above them. From the trees below came the hum of insects. In the distance a thin column of white smoke stood vertical; not a breath of wind. Jenny linked her arm into John's they gazed into the distance, living the peacefulness of that moment. Jenny closed her eyes. She felt the warm morning sun on her face and the warmth of John beside her.

"Wish Ross and Mary were here to share this." John turned to Jenny, gently stroking her cheek.

"You mean I'm not enough." She turned her face towards him, holding him with her soft gaze.

"You know what I mean, Jenny." He gave her a hug and stood up. "Come on." She gave him her hand and he pulled her to her feet. He picked up the backpack, and they continued up the path side by side.

"Ross has been funny the last few days, distant," John said.

"Pressure of work, John. That's what you were like most of the time."

"Did you mind?" he asked.

"Of course I mind."

"Then let's go hiking more often," he said, "or rock climbing."

As the evening drew in John scouted around for a good place to camp. The route had been steadily up hill most of the day. The return march tomorrow would be a breeze. He found a cleft in the rocks a few yards from a pool of clear water. They would be sheltered from behind, but with a clear view of the night sky above and over the plains beyond. He built a ring of stones on a bare rock and piled in dry deadwood, which blazed and quickly turned to glowing charcoal. They threw in potatoes to bake and set to work stripping thin branches to make skewers for the vegetables and meat, which they would barbecue later. After a day's walking, the water from the pool surpassed the best vintage of Californian wine, but you can only drink so much water. As dusk fell, they switched to bourbon and felt the warmth flow through them and the spirit come alive. The aches and pains of the day receded as the tide fell in the bourbon bottle, just like the tide in the ocean receding across the sand. As the meat spluttered on its spit, the stars began to glow faintly in the sky, and sharpened to bright points as the night darkened and the embers of the fire faded. As the fire died, the stars seemed to descend to just above their heads, almost to touch. They slipped into the sleeping bag, and with the discretion willingly accorded to young lovers, those magnificent heavens retreated and the man and woman became aware just of each other, very aware of each other.

***

Police work does not respect the Sabbath, and this Sunday morning was no exception. Once again Ross was in the Captain's office. This time he had to explain that he had been unable to get hold of John Ralphs. All he could do was leave messages on the answering machine, which he had done. The Captain told Ross that they were to be investigated, and this was why he wanted to see Ralphs. Given that he is on suspension, I would say they would regard it as open season on him, he told Ross. The investigating team were due to arrive on Monday, the next day, but in Ralph's obvious absence there was nothing for it but to get him in first thing on Monday and hope there was time for a briefing before the investigators arrived. The chances were that there would be, so that was the plan. Ross left, hoping desperately that John was only away for the weekend. Sure enough, he got hold of John on Sunday evening and agreed to pick him up first thing on Monday.

The Captain looked John Ralphs in the eye.

"Listen, Ralphs, I'm going to be frank. You're a suspect, so you're on suspension. It's worse than you think."

"How worse?"

"Don't interrupt, Ralphs. Listen. I've read Kinley's reports on you. They're good. Ross here is your lifelong friend. I'm new here. God bless Kinley and my sympathies go to his bereaved family. But I'm here. Shall I trust you?"

"You have my oath, Sir," John answered.

"Let me tell you both a story. This is personal. I'm here because the politicians screwed me. By politicians I mean the ones in the Police Department who pretend to be policemen. I told the truth and became a scapegoat. That's all you need to know. So you know what?"

"No, Sir," Ross replied, embarrassed by the course the conversation was taking.

"I'm going to act like a politician when I need to, to protect me, and to protect you. You know what that means?"

"It means you're going to take us into your confidence, Sir, when you know you shouldn't." The Captain was impressed by John Ralphs' perspicacity. Was this a bad or a good sign, he wondered? A shrewd policeman or a devious crook. Well, he had taken his choice, so he continued.

"If there's a bad apple in my department, it's me who gets him out, *not* the investigators. In fact, I just want to get him out. He can resign. I don't want to attach blame that will besmirch my department. Frankly, I don't see that serves the common good, not in my role as politician. Do you have a reason to resign, John?" he switched to first names. "Because if you do, resign now, and you are a free man, whatever you may have done." The only sound in the room was the three men breathing. John thought of his weekend in the hills, of the freedom. He thought of his friends who were dead.

"Sir, I can never resign as long as those bastards breathe freely the air of our town. Sir, all I've ever done wrong is to treat police time as my own when we had nothing going on, and I've repaid that many times over with my own time spent on police work." John held the Captain's stern gaze, and the Captain held his.

"I think you are vicious, devious crook, Ralphs." The Captain still held his gaze, but John did not flinch.

"I don't believe you, Sir."

"Well, it was worth a try," the Captain said. "Whether you are a crook or not, we'll pretend you aren't, but you should know that you're probably going to be accused. I'm going to protect the Department first and foremost. If I believe you to be innocent, I shall protect you, but that comes second to the Department."

"You've made yourself clear, Sir. But I'm innocent until proven guilty."

"I wouldn't be so sure about that, John. I've made myself more than clear. I've taken you and Ross into a confidence that is way over the line. Respect it." With that the conference was over. The Captain was motivated by an "enlightenment" learned from his past. This did not figure in Hadley's planogram, at least not yet.

An overwhelming sadness enveloped Jenny, when John told her of the meeting in the Captain's office. John, who had always stood up for what was right, who had devoted himself to his profession, often at her expense, this same man was to be accused, pilloried. Was this really how the idealism of youth transmuted into the worldly wisdom of middle age? I am still young, she thought. I can, and will, hold to my beliefs. This man cannot be crushed by the machinery of police bureaucracy, of any bureaucracy. I would not have strung my life on the line as he did when he stormed that warehouse, believing he was up against nine ruthless killers, and yet he did that for his sense of right, of responsibility for what he does. That is him. That is him as I see him, him as I know him. Then her anger melted as she thought of the confidence the

Captain had placed in John. Perhaps there was hope. I have to help him. The key must lie with Bill Hadley, with his hoodlum brother. Bill likes me. He will help me.

Bill Hadley was hunched over his laptop. He was feeding into his planogram, retrospectively, what actually happened. The raid on the jewel store did not readily fit the plan, as he had described it. It went so much better. I need to automate this, he thought, rather than having to reprogram the thing. I need to link my spreadsheets better. This was the start of a six hour session on the planogram, on its structure. Thoughts of all else vanished as he concentrated his energy on honing his tool, the planogram.

CHAPTER TEN

In the days that followed, Jenny found herself more and more drawn towards Diane, her psychiatrist's wife, a psychiatrist she did not really need, but then there were only a couple of sessions to go. Part of it was that Jenny had taken a couple of weeks of vacation "to recover", and without the normal routine of her office was at a bit of a loss as to what to do, especially with John mooching around like a lost soul these days. Diane was a breathe of fresh air, lively, but unlike Jenny, deeply cynical. Her enthusiastic style belied her ability to expose the dark side of life, always with humour.

Eventually the subject gnawing at Jenny had to come to the surface. They had consumed a light lunch, salad, at Juanita's and were sitting over the remains of a bottle of Chardonnay.

"I took your advice." Jenny smiled at Diane in expectation of recognition.

"I didn't know I gave you any advice," Diane responded with her habitual smile around the eyes, inviting Jenny to continue.

"The brother. I asked him. Hadley. About the brother. His brother."

"Jenny, you don't strike me as being particularly stupid and naïve, but I think you had better fill me in," Diane said. Jenny proceeded to describe how she had bought into the idea of Hadley having a brother, how she had gone to Hadley's office and how she had achieved confirmation of this fact. She then went on to explain how the police were having trouble tracking the brother down, given that they did not even have his name.

"Jenny, I gave Giles a tough time at your party, but he's not half as naïve as you," Diane said.

"What do you mean, naïve?" Jenny was taken aback.

"The logic, Jenny. Think of the logic." Diane poured herself another glass of Chardonnay and adopted a serious posture. "We know the voice exists. We know Hadley exists. We do not know his brother exists."

"But he told me," Jenny protested.

"Think, Jenny. What would he tell you if he was the bad guy?" Diane leant towards her and whispered, "my brother's a dirty rat." So Jenny, until you have proof of the brother's existence, Hadley is prime suspect in my book. I didn't say at the party that he had a brother. I just raised the possibility, principally because I wanted to get one over Giles in front of the rest of you, by bringing up a new idea he hadn't thought of."

"So what would you have done?" Jenny asked.

"I think you had better fill me in on the background, before I answer," Diane replied, and Jenny went on to describe how, from her perspective, everything had developed over the last few weeks. For Diane it was a dramatic and desperate story. She knew of the kidnapping but this story, told in full, was incredible. She asked Jenny to tell her more about the three characters they had identified, Bill Hadley, Jim Duggan and Bob Mitchell and what John and Ross thought about them.

By now lunch was well over and Diane suggested they take a walk.

"You know my husband's a psychiatrist," she said, "and I've learned a lot from him. Some of the weird situations he sees have weird solutions."

"Like what?" Jenny asked.

"No, let's keep to the point. I have another question. John says he saw a big guy outside the apartment when you were kidnapped, so he guessed it was Bob Mitchell. Right?" Diane waited for confirmation.

"That's what he thought," Jenny confirmed.

"But you had one kidnapper who was not a big guy. So how do we make that fit?" Diane turned her head towards Jenny as they walked and raised her eyebrows.

"It doesn't," Jenny said.

"Well, I say," Diane continued, "let's give John's hypothesis the benefit of the doubt. It simply means that the guy who picked you up in the street is not the same guy as your gaoler."

"I guess that works," Jenny agreed.

"OK, now this is where I said you were naïve. If Mitchell, or Hadley, are the bad guys, psychopaths maybe from what you tell me, you're wasting you're time going round to talk to them. They'll twist you round their little finger." Again Diane awaited Jenny's response.

"So what do you do?" Jenny asked.

"In my book, Jenny, you go round to their place, at least from what you've told me about Mitchell, and beat the hell out of them. You can't take a conventional approach with these guys. I'm sorry. This is not a very female approach." Jenny stopped, totally bemused, not quite understanding what it was that Diane proposed. She turned to Diane, not sure of what to say. Diane smiled at her, as if nothing were wrong.

"I'll tell you a little story about a little girl," Diane said.

To look at Diane, as she stood there before Jenny, you would scarcely credit the story she told, Diane the graceful, elegant psychiatrist's trophy wife. You know, she told Jenny, small town America has its surprises. She described how she would not be there if it were not for Giles. She had come to know Giles and not had one day's regret after their marriage five years earlier, despite, or maybe because of, the age difference. But that was all recent history, she told Jenny. In fact, she was born in Iraq. Her father was in the oil business and that was where he was posted for many years. She learnt fluent Arabic as a child and kept it up in her later studies. She described the fascination for her of the Iraqis, how they would love to hold her in the bazaar and ask to be photographed with her, for them a striking little blonde girl.

"And now you're going to laugh, Jenny." Diane paused, as if wondering how to put this and then continued, "The government of the United States decided I would make a good prostitute."

"They what?" Jenny retained her look of bemusement.

"The Gulf War. They wanted to infiltrate into Iraq women who might get close to Saddam. I was chosen." Diane grinned broadly.

"I don't believe you. You're joking," Jenny objected.

"I fit the bill, Jenny. The lingo. The looks. I had it all. They trained up five of us. Three went. They decided my psychological profile was wrong in the end. I don't know how the others got on."

"You are serious!" Jenny exclaimed.

"I am. And we had Special Forces training in unarmed combat. I still keep it up, but not on Giles, not yet anyway." Diane laughed. "So you see Bob Mitchell, all six foot six of him, all two hundred and eight pounds of him, to take the toughest of the three, is easy meat for me." They walked on while Jenny digested this information. She still did not appreciate what Diane was driving at.

"Jenny, what I am saying is forget the conventional approach. Assume we start with Mitchell, on the basis that he's the guy who picked you up, and therefore has it coming to him. If it turns out that he's a peaceful citizen, so be it: a casualty of war for the greater good. If he *is* a bad guy, then maybe we'll rattle them, and see where they go from there."

"Are you telling me, you volunteer to go round and beat the shit out of this guy, as they say in the police precinct?" Jenny was incredulous.

"It's better than the crap you tried on them, Jenny, as they say in the police precinct."

"I think Bill Hadley likes me, Diane. He'll help me."

"I'm sure he will, Jenny, and a lot more, maybe, if he's who we think he might be."

"You don't understand, Diane."

" I more than understand, Jenny. Forget it. Talk to Giles."

"I think your idea is crazy. If you're serious." Jenny was not sure now, what to believe about Diane. To be honest, she thought Diane's story at best to be exaggerated, embellished.

"Jenny, forget what I said. Just have another chat with Giles, before you do anything else." Diane had decided to use her special forces training after all. I shall just give him a playful little whack, she thought, just make a point, and see how he reacts.

From now on Jenny would only learn from Diane what she needed to know, and right now that was not very much. The only exception to the rule would be Giles. She had an obligation to him, her husband. This is small town America, she thought. If you take it upon yourself, America, to go around the world as a nation beating the shit out of exotic peoples, this is what you end up with, freaks like me. God bless America. Jesus. Giles is going to go crazy when he hears this. As Jenny took her leave of Diane, she failed to fathom the reason for the famous inscrutable smile, whether Sphinx or Mona Lisa.

That Giles would go crazy was an understatement, a very limited view of mankind's versatility. He reasoned with her, he begged her, he ordered her, he appealed to natural morality, to the civil code, to the founding fathers on the Mayflower and it was all to no avail. Just think of the stories you will be able to tell your grandchildren, she told him. I always knew my training would be of some value, other than protecting me against you, of course.

"I've decided on Mitchell, Giles. He's the toughest of the three. I like a challenge. Just think of him as one of my ex-lovers who's come to claim me back."

"Diane, you can't to this. This is the United States of America. We have laws." Giles was visibly upset, which was unusual for him.

"That's why I can do it, Giles. They trained me. I was quite good. Still am."

"What if he has weapons?"

"Then, Giles, I get the hell out of there, as fast as I can. Giles, if he has weapons, I'm dead meat." This was when Giles realised that she really was serious, that she had thought it through, that she was going to go in there and do her thing. He could not understand her. She had seen the trouble it had brought John and Jenny, trying to do something privately. This was why they had a police force, surely, to do the dirty work for them.

"Giles, calm down. Just think of it as a female remake of Terminator Two or Robo-she-cop." If nothing else, she knew how to wind him up.

The other thing that concerned Giles was that the name of Hadley had come up. He knew Hadley reasonably well. He felt it better to keep quiet about this for the moment. In Diane's current mood, she might change her mind and go after Hadley first. That would be embarrassing. He could imagine the scene of Hadley coming to see him and being introduced: *Mr Hadley, have you met my wife, Diane?* I may be a psychiatrist, he thought, but the female psyche continues to evade me.

"Ah well, Diane," he said, "I suppose there's always the possibility of divorce, if I want to exculpate myself from this madness." She laughed and smiled back at him.

"Giles, if you don't think our marriage can survive a couple of brawls I may wish to have with strange men behind closed doors, then I wonder why you married me to start with. Do you really think anyone would believe Mitchell, if he accused little old me of beating him to pulp in his own home? I don't think so." This looked as good a point as any to end the debate, so they did. It was also the case that Diane did not believe in procrastination, but she was nervous, so she retrieved her old combat notes and took care to differentiate between the lethal and the non-lethal moves.

***

Bob Mitchell was snoring on his sofa in front of a football game on TV, when the entry bell rang. The trashcan contained a couple of empty peanut packs and numerous beer cans. On the table was a half empty bottle of Bourbon and a half full glass. Bob had installed an entry video system to vet his callers. He liked what he saw, took a moment to tidy the place and pressed the entry buzzer. He moved to the door to let her in. Looks too classy for me, he thought. I like the shape though, slim, lithe, pretty eyes. I like her smile and yes, blonde is OK for me. The relevant word that did not occur to Bob was "disarming".

She walked in without a word. Circled his lounge and then took a seat, motioning to him to take a seat opposite. If there was anything unusual, it had not struck Bob yet. Nothing had struck him yet, but that would soon change. Diane had reconnoitred the flat on entry and established that there were no weapons visibly to hand, not surprising, but you never know, there could be an ornamental Samurai sword or whatever. It was unlikely, she thought, that he would routinely carry weapons on his person, and there were no suspicious bulges on him that she could see. She wanted to take this slowly, to leave a sense of menace, for when he thought about it afterwards. Silence. Bob Mitchell looked at her, but he was not sure of what to say. He felt tongue-tied like a kid at the annual ball. Surely she should say something: she must have come for a reason. Silence. He coughed.

Diane judged her moment. As he leant forward in his seat towards her to break the silence, her steel capped left shoe shot out catching him on the right shin with an audible crack. He automatically reached down in pain, and shock, and she grabbed his hair with both hands, smashing his head onto the glass coffee table, which shattered. So far no blood. She stood up, thinking, OK I've made my point, now he'll talk. But Bob Mitchell, tough guy used to inflicting pain, was not slow to react. He had not had Special Forces training. He had trained on the streets, and you can argue about which training is better.

This was the moment Diane did not want: escalation. He pulled from his boot a three-inch blade. She had underestimated this weapons freak. She wanted to speak, to back down, but he looked too grim. She circled anti-clockwise and he followed. Then, as she spun back clockwise, he had the impression she was retreating. Again her left foot flicked out, catching his right wrist and sending the blade flying into the corner of the lounge. In one movement Bob, agile for his two hundred and eighty pounds, somersaulted backwards over the sofa, grabbing her hair and pulling her down with him. She felt herself spin through the air like a rag doll, as his weight exerted its leverage upon her.

Even as they hit the floor, Bob had extracted his automatic from his shoulder holster. She felt the cold metal of the barrel rammed into her mouth as her head cracked against the oak frame of the bookcase. He has not had time to release the safety catch was the thought that came to her, as she brought her knee up into his groin and violently arched her back to pull her head clear of the weapon. The weapon was in his left hand. She grabbed his wrist with her right hand and smashed his hand into the glass door of the bookcase. She heard the thump of the automatic land on the carpet, curled her body into an unbelievable posture to at once rise to her feet, grab the weapon and hurl it, smashing, through the window. Bob had also regained his feet, by now disarmed, she hoped. She couldn't believe how he had come through that blow to the groin so fast, but she was already driving hard into his solar plexus and he went down. As he fell, she gave him a relatively gentle rabbit chop on the larynx, not to shatter it, but just to leave him sore. The final anaesthesia was a blow of the right foot to the left temple. Grunts but no words had been exchanged.

"Mr Mitchell," Diane said to his inert form, "this did not go the way I expected. I've never done this for real before. It's not like training, where you know the moves. To tell you the truth, I'm scared shitless, and I'm getting the hell out of here." This should never have happened. I wish I had listened to Giles, was her last thought as she left.

When he finally regained consciousness some minutes later, Bob was confused. He looked around him, surveyed the damage. His first thought was that he had been hitting the bourbon too hard. He saw the smashed bottle on the floor. Then he sniffed. There was a lingering scent of perfume, and he began to believe he really had had a visitor, an elegant blonde who packed a powerful punch. He called Hadley.

"Bill, the jeweller's exacting retribution. Three heavies just tried to do me over. I fought them off, but they've trashed the place. I'm gonna shoot that little shit. Let's meet." Without waiting for a reply, he hung up.

***

"But you're my wife." Giles' anguish hung on his words. He was seated in his study on a red leather armchair. Diane knelt at his feet on a Kashan rug. She had just related the events at Mitchell's place. "I hear this stuff from my patients. That's professional. But you're my wife."

"You know I trained with the Special Forces." She felt the easy sense of release from having told her story. The earlier tension had subsided.

"Yes, but I thought that was like evening classes, you know, Karate." Giles was mortified by what she had told him, by what she had done. "You entered a citizen's house with intent to beat him senseless, which is what you did. You don't do that, Diane."

"Giles, some innocent citizen! You name me an innocent citizen who pulls a three-inch blade from his boot and then rams an automatic down my throat." She was reliving the scene and flushed red with the memory of the exertion and danger.

"But that's not the point," he protested.

"That is the point. We now know this guy's guilty as hell, and by contagion the other two." She rose and moved towards the desk and the telephone.

"You can't tell Jenny," he said.

"I know, Giles." She felt everything slip away from her. "I hated every moment, just as you do. And I can't tell anyone. Only you. I didn't think of this. The reality is that there's still no evidence and anyone I tell is at risk *because I tell them*. So I must shut up…and regret what I did. I can't believe this is true. What go into me?"

She came across to him. Nestled herself against him, and the tears she had not learned in Special Forces training flowed freely.

As he held her against him, Giles began to visualise a contest, like a chess game. The Grand Masters were pitted against each other. It seemed Hadley, whom he knew, was one Grand Master. Who was Hadley's opponent? He thought about this. John had struck a posture; but not John against Hadley, he hoped. Jenny, even worse. Diane, please no, Diane who had just entered the fray. Or was it just Hadley against the system? He thought about Hadley, nice guy pleasant, intelligent. Maybe he should ask John, or Jenny, if this was the guy they mentioned who had raised the spectre of the psyschopath, when they came round to see him that time. Hadley, a psychopath? Unlikely. But then that was true of psychopaths. From what Diane had established today it was Hadley. It had to be Hadley. But *she* was crazy, with what she did today. Was she psychopathic? Was it Diane? He did not want to follow this line of thought. Diane had no idea of his thoughts, but she rose and left him, exhausted.

I am personally involved now, with what Diane has done today, he thought. So it has got to be Giles against the world. Who else can compete against whomever it may be, other than me? Dear god, let it not be Diane. I know it is not Diane. I have been married to her for five years. And? Would I have guessed that she would do what she did today? Is this Special Forces stuff really true? I never checked it. Maybe she was in an asylum, and lied to me. God, I am going mad. I must think, employ my training. He took a sheet of paper and wrote names at the top of each column, and then he began to fill in what he knew beneath each name. By midnight he realised that he knew very little. The names were first of all his friends, John, Jenny and Ross; then his acquaintance Hadley, followed by Duggan and Mitchell, Mitchell who had tried to kill his wife, or so she said. Do not get emotional, he decided. But as for Diane, he was not capable of putting her name at the top of a column. If it was Diane, then life was not worth living. I need more names, he told himself. Let it not be someone among these, among my friends.

CHAPTER ELEVEN

Bill Hadley sat in his office, perplexed, awaiting the arrival of Mitchell and Duggan. It did not make sense to him that the jeweller, who was ready to deal, should have struck out at Bob Mitchell, not at this stage. He was going to have to press Bob to make a clear identification of the three intruders who had attacked him. Bill was very aware of the significance of escalation. The point was that you never knew where it would lead. It wasn't the same thing as using violence during a raid. If Bob had shared Bill's view on escalation, he would never have drawn the blade and then the gun against Diane. Ultimately, this is what led to his wrong conclusions about who she was. It all happened so fast that he had no time to get any information about her.

It was clear from the moment Bob arrived that he was after retribution, that he felt humiliated. The three of them sat around Bill's conference table. Bill rose to make coffee, but also to create space for him to think, away from Bob's constant haranguing. He determined that without specifics, they would be wrong to make a move. He returned with the coffee.

"OK, Bob, we're all in this together. You've got to give me something more to make a decision. What did these guys look like? What did they say? How did they get in?"

No answer.

Jim, who had revelled in the opportunity of taunting Bob earlier, also fell silent.

"Come on, Bob. Just describe one guy." Bill tried to encourage him.

"OK, there was only one," Bob admitted.

"Just one guy?" Bill was surprised by this sudden admission.

"No. One gal." Bob looked very embarrassed.

"So you let her in and she tickled you too hard," Jim screeched.

"Yes, I let her in. Anyone would have. Even you, with your minute pecker, Duggan." Bob was resigned to declaring the facts. "She caught me off guard. Like we're just sitting there and suddenly, crunch, and there's broken glass everywhere."

"Spare us the detail, Bob." Bill was keen to defuse this and just get the facts. "No one can protect themselves against sudden unprovoked violence, that's why *we* use it. Stop giggling like a schoolgirl, Jim. What'd she look like?"

"Five eight, elegant, blonde. Not your street fighting type."

"No idea who she was. What'd she call herself?" Bill asked.

"Nothing. Not a word. She could have been the Swedish ambassador's daughter for all I know." Bob tried to delve into his memory for any clues.

"The silent type, huh." Still smirking, Jim eyed Bob up.

"Clothes? Jewellery? Vehicle?" Bill asked.

"Nothing, Bill. I got a pretty serious crack on the head. Franky, it's all a bit confused. Bill reached for the phone.

"You know what, Bob? I'm going to call the jeweller right now to ask if it was him?"

The reaction of the jeweller as to whether he was behind the attack on Bob was one of such abject terror that Bill was confident the jeweller's denials were true. Anyway, there was no logic to it. They were about to conclude a first class business deal together. The meeting closed with the knowledge that they had a very serious problem that they had not begun to understand. Was someone probing their defences? Who and why?

***

The next morning, over breakfast with Diane, Giles revised his position. She was suitably contrite, unable to believe she had been so stupid, so full of her own ego, to have tackled Bob Mitchell, as she euphemistically put it. The idea had seemed almost playful to her. She had seen herself upsetting Mitchell, having him back off from her and her wagging a warning finger as she left. But when the coffee table had smashed, everything had spun out of control. She felt guilty to the core.

"Forget it, Diane," Giles said, "What's done is done. But we've got to come clean with John, and Jenny."

"I'll call her now." Diane got up and moved over to the phone. She could get Jenny before work, if she called now. She suggested they meet for lunch at Juanita's.

The first to arrive at Juanita's were John and Giles. They had a couple of drinks at the bar, before moving to a table. Diane and Jenny arrived together. At lunch they all had one overriding interest: what to do about this crazy situation. Diane described to them her visit to Mitchell and how extreme Mitchell's reaction had been, to the extent of jamming a gun in her mouth. The least shocked by this was Diane herself, who had regained her confidence by now, and was just glad she had not lost any teeth or split a lip. She had never doubted that she had had the advantage of surprise.

Giles was disturbed when John related to them how suspicion was falling on him, and far from his suspension being lifted, it looked rather as if the investigation was about to intensify. Diane held to her position that Hadley and Mitchell had to be the prime suspects, given that they had no evidence for the supposed brother, except Hadley's word. Hadley was now tainted by the weapon touting Mitchell, rather than exonerated by him as his alibi – at least, we have a bit of a turn around there, she suggested.

Then Giles grabbed the reins. He repeated his earlier warning to John and to Jenny, that if they were the focus of a psychopath, they should seriously consider getting the hell out of there, and now, without delay. If John had known about the anonymous letters, he might have agreed. As it was, he recognised the threat to their personal safety, but felt they had a duty, as he had expressed to the Captain, to stay with this one. There was too much history, too much personal grief involved. He could not just walk away, and live with that afterwards. They debated courses of action, what they could do. In the end John prevailed. He felt that they had already exposed themselves to too much personal risk. This was a police matter, and should stay such, exclusively. He, John, would again request to be allowed back to work on the case, and maybe Giles would be invited to provide some support with psychological profiling.

Three hours later John was in an interrogation room with two special agents handling the investigation. They questioned him aggressively, and he was baffled as to why they kept reverting to a raid on a jewellery store which had taken place a hundred miles distant. He knew nothing about this, but somehow they seemed to be tying this into the bank raids here and the scene at the warehouse. He was outraged when they implied that he might have deliberately allowed the fire truck to escape, finally breaking down in tears as he was forced, yet again, to relive that moment when his friend Captain Kinley died beside him, shot in cold blood in the line of duty.

"Kinley died believing what I believed," he screamed, "that there were heavily armed men in the warehouse."

"Others saw the supposed hostages draw their weapons," they insisted.

"I repeat. When I saw a weapon in the hand of a hostage, I believed he had overpowered the other man. I issued instructions and raced for the hotspot, the warehouse."

"It wasn't the hotspot." The same point over and over again.

"It was to my knowledge," John was growing weary. "I was wrong. I still believe my actions at the time were right. I took over seamlessly from Kinley and did exactly what he would have done, not one second lost." The logic of this was not lost on his investigators, and each time John's answers conformed to the same pattern. They could not establish any weaknesses. They were doing their duty diligently, and were swayed in his favour by his testimony. Had they known about the anonymous letters, their position might have been different. It was a gruelling evening for John, but as he left, a reassuring clap on the shoulder raised his spirits more than words could have. On his return home that evening, Jenny noted a renewed vigour in his manner and revived spirits.

Giles was pleased to hear John on the line first thing next morning, suggesting they get together and he agreed. Giles assessment of John was that he was a very focused policeman, smart and on the ball. Giles felt that he had been dragged into this whole thing, and if he wanted to work with anyone, it was with John. John wanted Giles to call the Captain, informally, to capitalise on what John felt had been a good meeting with the investigators the day before. The problem was, as the Captain explained to Giles, that it was out of his hands. The Captain told Giles that he intended to stand up for John, and added, in confidence, that he had reason for his own serious concerns, but would give John the benefit of the doubt for the time being. Giles did not communicate the latter part to John, but made a mental note to himself.

"We've gotta do something, but we've gotta keep the girls out of it," John said.

"True but difficult," Giles replied.

"That was on hell of a thing Diane did. I've seen that guy. He's huge." John whistled.

"I caught the tail end of Vietnam, John. We were taught to do crazy things. But that was different. I still can't believe Diane flipped like that."

"Maybe that's it, Giles. She did it all here. She never went to the Gulf. She never lived it, and her training was never put into its proper context." John was thinking of some of the police trainees who would sometimes come up with off-the-wall ideas, entirely inappropriate to the situation."

"Yeah, well, I guess we've got it in us somewhere. Maybe the training just drew it closer to the surface. We're all tense. Friends gunned down. Jenny kidnapped." Giles looked up at John, decided to move on. "I've drawn up a list John. We are all on it, except me…and Diane."

"What list, Giles?"

"Suspects." Giles began to explain how he had worked on the list last night, writing all the pertinent facts beneath each name in a column. He gave John a copy.

"Your column looks very bad, John." John looked up at him.

"What do you mean?" John asked.

"I mean it could look like you're involved with them, from what we know." Giles looked meaningfully at John. "Show it to Ross. Ask him."

"It doesn't work if you don't trust me, Giles." John looked rueful.

"That's not what I said. We've got to live in the real world. Face it. You're being investigated. You've got to know what it looks like, to an outsider," Giles explained.

"The Captain?" John began to wonder what he might have said.

"Consider him an outsider, John. He's new." Giles' words reminded John of his awkward position. He had to do something.

"Diane dropped a rock in the pool, Giles. Let's see what the turbulence throws up. I've got to find a way to get to Hadley, a way to get evidence."

The difference between John Ralphs and Bill Hadley was that John Ralphs believed he had to search for evidence, while Bill Hadley believed he could manufacture it, or rather counterfeit it, and that was what he was doing right now.

Her first day back, Jenny had left for work at the usual time. Hadley saw her go, and as soon as John Ralphs left the apartment block, Hadley, accompanied by Duggan, moved in. John had been called out to enough break-ins to know that there was only so much you could do for security. He decided he would prefer to have a broken lock than a broken door, so he just had the one five lever lock. Not that the number of locks would have made much difference to Duggan, who required little more than a minute to work out what he needed to crack this lock.

They were looking for an innocuous, but incriminating item to leave at a future crime scene. Seeing photos of Jenny on the mantelpiece reminded Bill of the walks with her in the woods, and he felt a pang. He should keep her sweet. Maybe he could make a move once her husband was in jail. A photo, that would be good, he thought. Immediately identifiable as Ralph's wife, and with his prints on it. Was it plausible that you could lose a photo on a raid? What about in a wallet? On a neck chain, like a locket? In the pocket of a jacket, pulled off or ripped in the action? No, John would not be in the raid. He would be outside. Standing lookout? Or maybe we set him up to disturb us on the raid, but then they find evidence of his presence where it could not have been, that implicates him.

"Jim, we need some brainstorming here." Hadley continued to look around, while Duggan worked on a floor safe in a cupboard off the hall.

"I was thinking of shoe prints. That kind of stuff," Duggan responded.

"Difficult in a marble banking hall, Jim. What about leaving something in the getaway car? In the heat of the moment."

"I've got his police identity badge here in the safe, Bill." Jim's shrill voice intoned. A police badge, now that was something.

"What about his gun?" Bill asked.

"And his gun."

"Wow." Bill gave a soft low whistle. He pulled out his cell phone and called Bob, whispering hurried instructions. Ten minutes later Bob arrived with a very fat suitcase loaded with mineral water bottles filled with gasoline. Jim smelled the gasoline and gave Bill a questioning look.

"The problem is," Hadley said, "that if we take the gun and the badge, he will know as soon as he opens the safe. So we've got to burn down the apartment."

"That means the whole apartment block, Bill." Jim was not enthused by this idea. Bob sat there flicking his lighter expectantly. "I don't see us getting clear, Bill," Jim continued.

"So what's the alternative?" Bill also began to feel he was behaving precipitously.

It was Bob who answered. "Have Duggan unscrew the bolts holding the safe to the floor. I'll carry it out."

"How does that help?" Bill asked.

Bob again: "We do the raid before he realises. After the event no one will believe him. Two: even if he does report it, it's suspicious. Burglars steal the contents of safes, not safes, and this one's fifty kilos, at a guess."

"I buy that, Bob." Jim was quick to assent. "He had stuff piled on top to hide the safe. He won't know it's gone unless he goes to get something from the safe." Bill thought about this and agreed that it was a safer plan, if not as final as burning the place to the ground. He slipped one of the framed photos of Jenny into his pocket. Jim soon had the bolts free. He stood lookout while Bob carried the safe down the stairs and Bill carried the suitcase of gasoline, no longer required. Jim then set about leaving the apartment exactly as they had found it.

When John came home later the only thing that would strike him was an inexplicable smell of gasoline. He opened the windows to air the apartment.

CHAPTER TWELVE

A Tuesday morning like any other? Ten forty-five a.m. and John Ralphs heads north. His plan? To confront Bill Hadley again, following the episode with Diane and Bob Mitchell. As he leaves the town limits, a pick-up passes him, heading south with Hadley, Mitchell and Duggan.

"OK." As ever Bill is doing a quick recap. "The plan is to leave bullets in the bank, for forensics to examine, and the badge outside in the dust."

"Bob, you have Hadley's gun?" Bill asked.

"I have the gun in my left jacket pocket," Bob confirmed.

"And you have the badge, Bob?" Bill's second question.

"Sure, in my right jeans pocket, Bill. All set."

John Ralphs did not find Hadley at his office and decided to head on further to the farmhouse, another twenty miles. If he is not there, I shall try the office again on the way back, he told himself. By this time Ross was already taking statements from witnesses at the bank.

"Take it slowly," Ross said. The new manager was extremely nervous. He had never experienced a bank robbery in his life. Since he had been in this town he had already had two, the wild, wild west. Let me out of here was the one thought circulating in his brain. Hence the incoherent testimony.

Ross: "So you see this guy come in, looks suspicious."

The Manager: "Yeah, the big guy. I got no reason to, but I just buzz the alarm."

Ross: "And then?"

The manager: "He pulls out his weapon. Bang, aim, bang, aim bang, aim, bang. Just like that. Three shots."

Ross: "You say like he aimed at something or someone?"

The manager: "It was just like left, right, centre, into those two desks and the counter."

We'll retrieve those bullets, Ross thought, at least something.

The manager continued, calmer now in the same way as he had calmed down after the shooting. "He turned and bolted through the entrance. I skipped round the desks after him. I tell you I was petrified when I first saw him. Now he was on the run. And me? Like a dog yapping at his heels once he turns his back."

"So you followed him?" Ross questioned.

"Right out the door. He turned up the street on the left. Reached the vehicle. Some other guy came out of the doorway. They collided, fell, got to their feet. Truck door opened, and they were off."

"What truck?" John asked.

"Don't know. Black. Smoked glass." Ross signalled to one of the officers to check out where the truck was, while others continued to cordon off the area. The officer had a bemused look as he returned to Ross. He was holding something. Strange coincidence, it was where they collided and rolled in the dust, he told Ross, as he handed Ross a police badge.

The black truck did not go very far. It stopped close to John Ralph's apartment block. The three men slipped round the building. While Duggan checked Ralphs' apartment was empty, Hadley opened his truck, parked in front of the building, and Mitchell humped the safe up the stairs. Nothing looked disturbed, so they reinstalled the safe. The only missing contents were one police badge and three bullets from the gun. These would not be missing long. They had already been retrieved by the police. Even if the neighbours had heard the three men roaring with laughter as they descended the stairs, they would never have guessed why.

Ross was desperate to get hold of John, who had some mega-serious explaining to do. He called Jenny at work, but she had no idea where he was. He went in to see the Captain and told him about the badge. The Captain's instructions were clear.

"Do one thing, Ross. Get to him first. Talk to him. Bring him to me."

An hour later John was surprised to find Ross leaning against the door of his apartment. For the moment Ross played it cool.

"Hi, John. Can I come in?"

"Yeah, come on in. Lunch? Just tried Hadley. No luck." John seemed relaxed to Ross. Innocent or one hell of an actor.

"Where's your badge, John?" Ross went straight to the point, but gave him a chance for an explanation.

"I'm suspended Ross. I can't use it. It's in the safe with my gun."

"Show me," Ross instructed, and immediately regretted his words, as he thought of the gun in there. He reached for his holster automatically. John moved to the hall.

"Why do you want it, Ross?" John asked.

"Trust me, John," Ross replied. "Just give me that badge and your gun and I'll explain." However strange this may have seemed to John, he did trust Ross, and bent down to unlock the safe. He did not see the badge immediately. Ross, edgy, bent down, saw the gun and reached for it.

"Thank you, John." He slipped it into his pocket. John continued to fumble around in the safe.

"It's not here, Ross." Not what Ross wanted to hear, but what he expected.

"You'd better come with me. The Captain wants to see us. I'll explain on the way." In the end Ross preferred not to explain on the way. And when the Captain, carefully holding John's gun in a cloth, examined it and established that three bullets had been fired, Ross was glad he had kept quiet, was glad he had arrived safely at the Captain's office.

Of the three men in the room, John, the accused, was most at ease. He knew he had not taken part in a bank raid that morning, just as he knew that his badge had been in the safe and his gun had been in the safe. There had to be an explanation. So this looked like evidence but it was only circumstantial, damning yes, on the face of it, but circumstantial and wrong. As to the Captain, the Captain saw one of his officers before him, a man who had dropped his badge at the crime scene, who had hidden his gun in his safe, no doubt intending to deal with it later, and who now sat there, cock-sure. There could be no other explanation. You had to be hard-bitten to sit there as calmly as he did. A major scandal on my watch, he thought, when I'm in charge. It's all happening again, to me. For Ross it was worse: this was his best friend, or so he had thought. But no, he was a member of a ruthless gang that gunned down their friends, and he was still with the gang even after that. His consternation was turning to revulsion.

Engrossed in their thoughts, none of them heard the door open. It was the manager of the bank, now recovered from his ordeal, his statement duly signed and filed.

"Just wanted to thank you, Captain. I'm finished. Your guys did a great job. Hey, John. Didn't see you around for a few days. You missed the action, right?"

"You saw him this morning." Ross blurted out.

"What?"

"At the bank." Ross clarified.

The manager didn't hesitate for a second. "Only guys I saw, were a couple of clients, the big guy who ran out and the little guy he banged into." A fault line developed in Hadley's planogram.

"Outside," Ross insisted.

"Like I said, the big guy and the little guy. Not John. If you were there, John, I didn't see you." He left with a wave. Ross and the Captain looked at one another. Credibility built up over years can be destroyed in one second, and for them John's credibility had been destroyed with the examination of the gun, but now maybe it hadn't. But it is not so easy to recover, so easy to climb from the bottom of the pit as to slip into it. Suspicion was firmly rooted.

"The eyewitness exonerates you, John," the Captain said.

"It's his badge, his gun, his bullets," Ross objected.

"That's the problem," the Captain said. "You see the problem, Ralphs?" John remained silent. He did see the problem looming very, very large.

"In a small town like this we can hide a lot of stuff." The Captain looked at the gun on his desk. "I asked you before if you want to resign. Do you?" Ross gasped at the Captain's words, at the thought that this man could be allowed to go free in the face of the evidence against him.

"I do not resign, Sir." John's answer was as clear and firm as the Captain's question was grave.

The Captain thought about what he had been obliged to live through before: the character assassination, the slander, the lies, the recrimination, and above all the disastrous consequences for the policing of the community. Was this man guilty? If he were innocent this whole dreadful process would take place anyway. They would all be ruined. And if he were guilty? Well maybe they would just have to catch him another way. If the bank manager denied to the court that Ralphs was present at the raid, then as far as a court was concerned, he was not present. The badge and the bullets alone would not convict him, but if he were innocent, they might have destroyed his life by the time the truth came out. And mine too, he thought. With an air of resignation he picked up the gun and handed it to John. Then he passed across the badge.

"You must have dropped this. Ross, please go with John to check his apartment. Look for signs of forced entry."

Ross was morose, as they drove to the apartment. John racked his brains for an explanation. Suddenly he turned to Ross. "Hey, Ross. You want proof of where I've been. Well I must have done a hundred miles this morning."

"What does that prove, John?"

"I had my car serviced yesterday. Picked it up late. They'll have written down the mileage. Check it now. See how far I went." John was excited to have something.

"You could have driven all night, John." Still glum, disinterested.

"But I didn't. Come on, Ross. Maybe it's not conclusive, but it's something." John was adamant and Ross reluctantly agreed that putting together fragments could build a picture. In the apartment they had less success, until Jenny came home. In response to John's question of whether anything was out of place, she pointed out that a picture was missing from the top of the side cabinet.

"This may not say much for my house-keeping, Ross, but you can see the dust mark," she said. And sure enough you could. John then recalled the strange smell of gasoline, but that did not get them anywhere. For John they had drawn a blank. For Ross dark suspicions remained, as well as the feeling that the Captain had done the wrong thing this time.

***

Bill Hadley, Jim Duggan and BobMitchell had separated in town, but they came together in the evening at the farmhouse for a celebratory dinner, which in this case meant Chinese take-outs and beer.

"Some things go better than planned," Bill said. "I can't believe we got that safe back in place."

"Wouldn't have worked if we burnt the place down," Jim retorted.

"Jim, you were right. Congratulations." Bill toasted him, taking a swig from a can of beer. "The badge will lead to the gun, and the gun shot the bullets."

"Yup, right into the woodwork," Bob laughed. "Easily retrieved, undamaged. Goodbye, Mr Ralphs, sorry, Lieutenant Ralphs."

"She's yours for the taking, Bill." Jim had seen Bill slip the photo of Jenny into his pocket, when they burgled the apartment.

"What's next?" Bob enquired.

"We lay low. Let forensics take its course. They'll charge him."

Bill fell silent. The next move was not clear to him. "Give it a few days, boys. Let's think about it." He wanted to expand the organisation. Maybe it was time. He needed to make a move on the woman too, settle that one way or the other.

"I still don't know about the blonde." Bob broached the remaining unsolved issue.

"What blonde?" Jim asked. He knew. He just wanted to force Bob to say it.

"My visitor, Jim, my visitor." It was true. She did not fit into the pattern anywhere. Having an elegant blonde come round and beat the shit out of you was not just coincidence, and none of them believed in coincidence anyway.

"I forgot about her," Bill admitted. "Easier for me than for you I guess, Bob. Your intimate relationship and all that."

"Painfully intimate, for several days," Bob said. "She's gotta be someone. You find out, let me know. I'd like to meet again. On my terms."

At that moment Diane was with her husband Giles, who had accepted John's urgent request to come round as soon as he could. Giles had picked up the urgent tone in John's voice, when John left the message on Giles' answer machine. The four of them, John, Jenny, Giles and Diane, were huddled round the kitchen table, heads together like good old fashioned anarchist conspirators in Europe of the late eighteen hundreds. So much for John's idea of keeping the girls out of it and leaving it to the professionals, to the police.

John related to them the curious tale of the badge and the gun. Then he suggested he withdraw for a few minutes while they discussed it. If they believed him, they should call him back into the kitchen. Otherwise Giles and Diane were free to go. He did not doubt that Jenny believed him. Among the three of them, the strong advocate for John's case was Diane. Her belief was based on her experience with Bob Mitchell. Diane had no doubts that Mitchell was a crook, and she simply could not see John in the same camp as that guy. Giles tried to retain professional detachment but in the end he had to agree with her. Jenny voted for John, and with a unanimous vote they called him back in.

Giles suggested that they needed a framework to think the situation through. He gave each of them his list of suspects, striking a line through two columns, one headed *John* and the other headed *Jenny*. Jenny requested that they concentrate on Hadley first, and this was when Giles learned that Hadley was the man who, in this very room, had broached the subject of psychopaths. He was the man who had prompted John and Jenny to raise the subject with Giles. Now they considered the fact that they knew that Hadley was associated with Mitchell, and Mitchell was a man who bore arms in the privacy of his own home, as Diane had established. Giles could not resist pointing out that Mitchell had grounds for bearing arms, if guests like Diane were likely to turn up. This elicited her objection, on the grounds that bearing arms had not done Mitchell much good against her.

Giles listed a summary of Hadley:

Hadley with the voice of the man at the warehouse. A brother? (*According to Hadley alone*).

Hadley with the two alibis: one, Mitchell, a crook? Duggan?

One man plus two alibis is equivalent to three men at the warehouse.

Jenny questions Hadley and is kidnapped.

Hadley, not even an acquaintance, visits the Ralphs after the kidnapping.

Hadley raises the subject of psychopaths.

Not as bad as John's profile, according to the police.

"That's it," Giles said.

"So let's take a look at the idea that he's framing me," John proposed.

"Any evidence for that?" Giles asked.

"The Captain. I'm sure he knows something he's holding back on. Maybe Ross too." John thought of the meetings where it was suggested he resign.

"I'll probe that tomorrow, John." Giles offered. He would find a reason to meet the Captain, perhaps offer his services on the case.

Diane: "How do we take the next step with Hadley?" Silence.

"What would the police do, John?" Diane asked.

"Probably not your approach with Mitchell." He grinned at her. "Surveillance, I guess."

Giles: "Can we do that?"

"I don't think so," John replied.

"But I could meet him," Giles suggested. " He knows me."

"To find out what?" Jenny asked.

"We're going in circles," John said. "This happens."

"The badge and the gun. Anything there?" Diane addressed the group.

"And the photo," Jenny said, and remembered she had not told them about the missing photo.

"So let's keep Hadley as prime suspect," Diane stated. "He enters your apartment, takes the gun and the badge, returns the gun after the raid and takes the photo."

Giles: "How does he get into the safe, twice?"

John thought about this. "Same way as he gets into the flat. Lock's no obstacle. Knows what he's doing. Leaves no trace. Jenny's at work. I'm out at Hadley's, but Hadley's raiding the bank. Puts the gun back before I return. It works, but why does he want the photo?"

It was Jenny's turn to think, and then she came out with it. "If he's the kidnapper, well, he was very courteous, but to be honest the walks in the woods were weird. I kind of felt he wanted me to talk. I did. I was lonely."

Giles took up the point. "It would help explain why he came to see you afterwards. He might have wanted to justify himself to you. That's why he tried to explain a psychopath's way, his way. That would mean that he knows himself for what he is. That's doubly dangerous."

"That still doesn't help us with an action plan, Giles, and that's what we need," Diane objected.

"You're right, Diane, but if we can work him out, crack his psyche, then when something happens we'll be able to pin it on him, link him in."

"I agree with you, Giles." John looked at each of them. "That's what we try to do. If his motive lies in his psychological make up, then we're a big step forward."

"You mean, like, you can predict him?" Jenny asked.

"Only if we are very, very clever," Giles answered for John. "And we are. A combined IQ of what? Five to six hundred?"

"You must have missed me out, if that's all you get, Giles," Diane said with a laugh, and proposed that they move on to John's bourbon, and give the grey cells a chance to ferment.

The Captain was responsive to Giles' request for a meeting the next day. He had not really settled into the town. The situation he had parachuted into was dire and was taking all his time. Social life was non-existent. Meeting the psychiatrist would be for him much missed relaxation in pleasant company, an interlude in his heavy work schedule. Giles had met the Captain a couple of times. As he drove there, he was wondering how to play it. When it comes down to it, we need the protection of the police. This idea of investigating privately is mad. If they kidnapped Jenny just for talking to Hadley, what the hell would they do to Diane when Mitchell found out who she was? He could not bear to think. Gradually a plan formed in his mind. If I can hook the Captain on this idea, he thought, if I can just hook him.

The Captain was courteous and welcoming. He barred all calls and ordered coffee. Giles declined biscuits. The two men eyed one another, the one welcoming, the other apprehensive. Giles felt much was at stake, and he was not sure where to begin. Social chitchat soon ran dry. Empathy, Giles thought. I'll try empathy.

"You have lot on your plate," Giles opined.

"Couldn't be worse. Three bank raids. Armed. Homicide. One officer on suspension. And I'm new here."

"Do they give you help?" Giles asked.

"Hindrance. Investigators. Questions. All that stuff."

"Can't you fix the suspension?" Giles was leading in the direction he intended to go.

"Out of my hands, but I think it's over now."

"I've come round to believing John." This was news to the Captain, that they had been speaking. "John thinks there's something you're not telling him."

"Anonymous crap. I binned it."

"Isn't that evidence or something?" Giles was surprised that such material should be discarded.

"Giles." The Captain looked at him meaningfully. "Yes, it is. The truth is I have more than enough crap on my hands already, as you said earlier. Personally, I'm not sure I do believe John, but I'm not having my department ripped apart in an investigation that goes nowhere."

Giles gave an understanding laugh and asked whether the Captain had time for his comments on the situation, in the sense of helping not interfering. The Captain agreed. Giles then launched into his monologue.

"In my view we're not talking about hoodlums hitting a bank. Two things strike me: planning and ruthlessness. To me the whole thing has the hallmark of a madman, and that's not John. If our man is a psychopath, and let's assume he is highly intelligent, he can focus his mind on his work in a way that you and I would love to, but can't. How do you catch a psychopath?" It was a rhetorical question, but the Captain answered it.

"We don't. We wait till his overconfidence trips him up."

"Exactly," Giles continued. "I'm going to test out a hypothesis on you now. Let's call our man Bill. Bill raids a bank. For whatever reason Bill sees John's wife as a threat and snatches her. Maybe he wants to frighten John, force John to back off or whatever, but he changes his plan and releases her. Maybe he gets fixated on her. We'll keep that idea for later. Now I come to the really strange thing. You find John's police badge at the next crime scene. John says the badge was in his safe. Think about it. John's on suspension, so he has no reason to carry his badge anyway, and certainly not when he goes on a bank raid."

"So he's being framed is what you're telling me."

"What I'm telling you is that it has all the hallmarks of a very clever guy manipulating the situation. Also there's something you don't know."

"What's that?" the Captain asked, intrigued by the course Giles' argument was taking.

"John found no signs of a break-in at his apartment, but a photo of his wife was missing. She noticed it. You heard what I said about a fixation. There's a second thing you don't know. Shall I tell you? Mitchell, one of Hadley's alibis, stinks. Carries lethal weapons."

"How do you know that?"

"You don't want to know," Giles answered. "Maybe I'll tell you one day when I get to know you better. It's not anything you can use as evidence."

"So there's a reason why you chose the name *Bill*."

"You've got it. It's a serious accusation, so let's call it a hypothesis for now." Giles grinned at the Captain. "I was wondering on the way over here, if it's possible to set a trap. Why I think it might be possible is because Bill thinks he's got us. If we let him continue to believe this, we can lead him into a trap."

"What's the trap?"

"I don't know, but let me make another point before we get onto that. First, John is not at risk from Bill. He's not at risk, because Bill wants to frame him for the bank raids."

"And jewellery raids, by the way," the Captain cut in. Giles raised his eyebrows and noted the information, before continuing.

"Jenny is probably not at risk now. I think she is very much at risk, once Bill has had John convicted of his crimes. Unfortunately, my wife Diane is very much at risk."

"What the hell's she got to do with it?" The Captain sat back astonished.

"Let me just say, she's the one who fingered Mitchell." Giles thought fingered was as good a euphemism as any, in the circumstances. After a few seconds silence, Giles continued, "Somehow, I want it to be clear to Hadley that Diane enjoys the protection of the police. Maybe you can find a way of employing her, get something in the local paper. This is a personal request. Please think about it."

"I will." The Captain pondered the implications of what he had learned from Giles this morning. The Captain continued, "The first thing that is clear is that John has to stay on suspension, so that *Bill*, as you call him, believes his plan is working. Well, that's the only thing that's clear."

"I think there is one other thing," Giles said. "This man is highly focused on his plan. This is the plan he is executing right now. Therefore he has to do something. He won't just wait. We need to know what he is going to do, so we need bait."

"We need bait," the Captain repeated. "I think we're going to have to mull this one over."

CHAPTER THIRTEEN

Bill was intrigued to read in the Herald and Courier that the police had appointed a special investigator. At last they're getting on with it, he thought, and then smiled when the significance hit him: they had to bring in a special investigator, because suspicion lay on one of their own. He looked admiringly at the picture of her. Later that morning the phone rang. It was an unusually excited Bob Mitchell.

"It's her. You seen the paper?"

"I don't know what you're talking about, Bob." Bill continued to type into his laptop.

"This woman in the paper. She's the one who came round here."

"I'm not clued up on your women, Bob." Bill continued typing.

"The one who laid into me, Bill." Bill understood, and immediately thought this was the opportunity to throw Bob to the wolves, but then remembered he had used Bob as an alibi.

"I'll think about it, Bob. They haven't got anything, but we'll think up some kind of subterfuge." Bill hung up.

The next day a letter arrived for the attention of the special investigator, and it was immediately delivered to the Captain.

Dear Madam,
I write to seek an explanation from you on behalf of my friend Bob Mitchell. He is reluctant to write for reasons that you may appreciate.

We are baffled.

Arriving at his house with my video equipment, I saw you leaving. We recognised your picture in the Herald and Courier today. I found Bob out cold, his lounge in disarray. He has limited memory of what happened, but believes himself to have been subjected to an unprovoked personal attack by you. Now he is worried that you will construe against him the fact that he was armed at the time.

I wish to point out that Bob and I are home movie aficionados. I was coming to his house to shoot a scene in which he was playing a Russian agent. The plot required him to conceal weapons on his person. The entire sequence was planned to be filmed in his house.

I know Bob to be a law-abiding citizen, and am baffled by this apparently extraordinary situation. My immediate intention was to write to your superiors, but Bob persuaded me to allow you the opportunity of an explanation.

Jim Duggan.

The Captain smiled, as he read the letter. The two alibis, he said to himself, and, of course, the mysterious threat to Giles' wife that Giles did not wish to talk about. How many psychopaths do we have around here? I think I am as baffled as Jim Duggan claims to be. He screwed the letter up and slung it in the bin. We already have one officer on suspension. Let's not have our fictitious special investigator fictitiously suspended. He called in Ross.

"Ross, the suspicion's back on Hadley, the man with the right voice. Our hypothesis is that he wants to frame Ralphs. Got that?"

"Yes, Sir."

"So I'm keeping Ralphs on suspension, even though they cleared him yesterday."

"To mislead Hadley?" Ross asked.

"Exactly. Talk to Ralphs. I want you to work with him, on the quiet. Don't tell anyone else."

Ross left the room and a huge weight fell from him. For the first time in weeks he felt normal.

The days had again been dragging for John Ralphs. Inertia,

boredom, you name it, he had it. He was surprised to open the door and see Ross standing outside. Ross shook his hand and congratulated him as he came in. He then filled John in on the situation. Giles had told John that he thought things were looking up for him, but this was excellent news. As they talked it over, the phone rang. It was Giles.

"John, I've talked to the Captain. Now you're in the clear we can see about what to do. I suggest we meet. All of us."

"Including Ross?" John asked.

"Especially Ross. He's our legitimation, as long as you're on suspension. Four today. Here." Giles hung up. Ross suggested they head out of town for a break and some lunch, before going across to Giles. John improvised a hamper from the fridge and packed it in a backpack.

They parked the car in the shade under some trees and headed out on a path that extended endlessly across the plains. The horizon was almost a full circle, broken only by the hills they had just come through. Just half an hour south of town and it was total peace. The sky above was clear with a few stray white clouds. They walked in silence, enjoying the freedom of the open countryside. They chose a cluster of trees to stop for lunch. John spread out on a cloth the contents of the backpack, bread, ham, cheese, fruit and mineral water. Finally, John broke the silence.

"You know it's down to you and me. The others are well-meaning."

"But they don't know police work." Ross completed the sentence for him.

"We should use Giles," John added. "Get his insights into Hadley."

"And then what do we do," Ross asked.

"If Hadley thinks he's got it figured, that has to be his weak point," John replied.

"Why?"

"Because he doesn't know we know." John fell silent and considered what he had just said. "Problem is…that doesn't get us anywhere." He packed the bag. They stood and set off back to the car. It was as if they had all the time in the world: they just did not know how to structure that time to trap Hadley, if it was Hadley.

In Giles' office it was John who took charge this time. Now that he was suspended only in appearance, he was the senior officer. John sat at the head of the table with Ross on his right, Giles on his left and Jenny and Diane on either side at the foot of the table.

"This is police work from now on," John opened. "That means that we will consult with you, Giles, as appropriate in line with the course of the investigation. Jenny, Diane, we will interview you as appropriate, but I'm sure you'll be pleased to hear that your roles are limited to that. As far as the world and the rest of the police department are concerned I am still suspended. Therefore Ross will act as my liaison. I report to the Captain. I'd like to thank you all for your confidence in me and your help."

"Well," Giles said, "I think the ladies can leave. Diane, you look relieved."

"I truly am. Come on, Jenny." Diane stood up and she and Jenny left together.

"That's one way of making friends," Giles said with a benign smile. "So what do you want?"

"What's Hadley's next move?" John asked.

"I think you can prompt it, John," Giles said. "As long as you are the prime suspect you're safe from him. He wants you to carry the can. And Jenny's safe until you're in jail. Play the Jenny card."

"What do you mean," John asked cautiously.

"Rile him, threaten him," Giles suggested.

"And what's that about Jenny?" John looked at Giles questioningly.

"If he took the photo, then he might be developing a fixation. Make him jealous. Make him do something stupid." Giles did not like giving this advice, but it looked like the most efficient way forward. John did not like receiving this advice, but he appreciated its merit."

"OK. Come on, Ross. Let's go." John looked at Giles. "We'll get the bastard now. Thanks, Giles."

"Oh, and John. While you're talking to Hadley, try and work out a way to bait the trap." These were Giles' parting words.

No time like the present, John thought, as Ross dropped him off. He walked across to his car. As John drove north to Hadley's office, he had time to think about how he would tackle this. He had to be careful not to raise suspicions, but at the same time, somehow or other he had to hook Hadley into a conversation and get him to give something away. It struck him that he should act as if he wanted Hadley on his side. If Hadley really had a fixation on Jenny, wouldn't he go for this? A chance to see her? Get closer? And the bait. What could the bait be. Well, he would have to play that by ear.

The first thing that struck John was the affable manner in which Hadley received him. Was he just very cool under fire, or was it something else?

"You were kind to show concern for us, Mr Hadley."

"Call me Bill," Hadley responded with warmth.

"I need help. Your brother."

"Nothing came of the photo I gave your colleague?" Hadley asked.

"The truth is, Bill, I'm not working at the moment. An internal problem." John cast his eyes down as if embarrassed by his admission.

"Why were you investigating me, John?"

"I guess it was because of your brother. Don't worry. Jenny's set my mind at rest about you. Said she couldn't for one second believe anything bad, after she met you here, and then you came round." Hadley listened to John and for a moment his eyes flashed.

"I'd like to help you and Jenny, John. I don't know how, but I would." Hadley reached across to shake John's hand.

"If I can't straighten this out, I'm leaving the police," John said, acting as if seeking sympathy. You bet you are, Hadley thought.

Jailbirds don't get to keep their jobs.

John continued, "All I ask for now is that you think about it and let me know of any ideas."

I will, Hadley thought, ideas that hasten your prosecution. You drivelling idiot. You're playing right into my hands.

"Thanks for coming, John. I'm glad there are no hard feelings. I will help." Short but sweet, Hadley thought, as he showed John out.

Thirty minutes later Bob Mitchell and Jim Duggan arrived. Bob was feeling good. He had just returned from the shooting range, where he had scored a personal best. He walked in and gave Hadley a hearty punch on the shoulder, before moving across to the fridge and extracting three beers, passing two to the others. Hadley motioned to them to take a seat and started to speak even as they sat.

"It's looking good. This guy's gonna take the fall for us."

"So we hit a few more banks before they take him in?" Jim asked in his off-key whine.

"It's time to build an organisation." Bill thought this was so obvious that he was moving straight on, when Bob interrupted.

"Build a what? You crazy? That costs money."

"We've got to use our potential, Bob," Bill said calmly.

But Bob was not calm. "I don't make money to spend on some organisation, which is always there and always wants money."

"We make more money, Bob."

"You got it wrong, Bill. Forget it." Bob was adamant. "My share's one third, whatever. I spend it."

"Your share's one third of what we make as three, not when we make more," Bill reasoned.

"One third. Period." Bob drew his gun and slammed it on the table.

"Have it your way. One third of what I do with you. I'm working other deals." Bill slid Bob's gun back across the table. There was no argument to this, but Bob glowered at Bill.

"I'm with Bob," Jim said. "Anyone else hears what I do, I'll tell

Bob to shoot 'em. There are six ears here, and six ears it stays. Never am I looking inside a prison cell."

"We have a class circus act," Bob said. "We do our thing. No one lives to tell the tale, and that's the way it stays."

"I'm the leader here," Bill started.

"You ain't no goddamn leader," Bob interrupted. "You're the planner. Day you stop planning, Jim and me plan. You got that?" Bill was thrown by Bob's vicious, derisive tone, and by Jim's nodded agreement.

"I can't believe you guys. I put this together," he started, but saw a rock face in front of him and stopped. "You're right we don't need no organisation." These bastards are dead meat, as soon as I can afford to ditch them, Bill thought.

Watching Bill, Bob's thoughts were different: he's going out of control, so I'll watch him, and when he's no use – bang, bang. He picked his gun up off the table and holstered it. Bob had few illusions about Bill's mental stability, despite Bill's outward appearance of calm.

Bob took the floor. "Bill, you got some planning to do. Me and Jim, we like what you do here. Right, Jim?"

"Right." Jim moved to the fridge for more beers.

"We got cash, mucho dinero. Right, Jim?" Bob glared at Jim.

"Right."

"Bill, we do stuff. We don't sit on our arses. We lie low here. OK."

"So what do you want?" Bill asked.

"Planning, Bill. We do something somewhere else. Right?"

This man truly does not know me, Bill thought. He dares to treat me like his flunky. Bill seethed inwardly. Bob grabbed another beer and smiled winningly at Bill. Bill's smart, but he can't control himself, he judged. He's easy meat when it comes down to it. Still, his special skills are very valuable to me for the moment. He laughed inwardly, and passed a beer across to Jim. To hell with them, Jim thought. When the shit hits the fan, I'm outta here, like yesterday, and it will hit the fan, with these jerks, one day, one day soon. As if to presage this turn of events, Jim stood up and walked through the door, flicking the lights off as he went.

"I'm outta here," he called back to them, where they sat in the dark.

In the darkness of her bedroom, Diane nuzzled against Giles. She felt warm and content: she did not feel like a special investigator of the police, but then again maybe it had its advantages.

"I'm investigating you, Giles," she whispered. "A very special investigation." He prepared himself for the investigation, which proved long and arduous, as she extracted all he had to give. Finally, he submitted and she relented, confessing it was just a training exercise and not the real thing.

"You know, Giles, that guy has a hold over Jenny," she said.

"I know. He's manipulative. He can spot what she needs and exploit it."

"And John?"

"She'd never have married him, if he exploited her like that. No offence meant to Jenny, but with Hadley, it's like giving a kid sweets and saying to her get into my car."

"You mean she's weak."

"I mean she's nice."

"I understand, Giles. I'm not nice?"

"To that you know the answer, Diane. I'll say it anyway. No."

"You didn't have to tell me, Giles." She gave him a kiss. "Jenny's going to be the bait."

"You're right. Come what may. She is." Giles gave a deep sigh, and then, succumbing to the effects of the earlier *interrogation*, fell asleep.

CHAPTER FOURTEEN

"The ball's in my court," John said to Jenny. "Hadley clearly thinks I've reached the end of the line."

"So what's he going to do?" Jenny asked.

"Once I'm in jail, ask you to marry him."

"John!" Jenny turned red.

"I'm serious, Jenny. You have an admirer." He smiled at her.

"It's worse, John. He has power over me. I feel it." She blushed. "I don't mean like I'm interested in him. It's different. It's like, well, like your favourite actor. It's hypnotic."

"I guess that's part of why he likes you, Jenny. He sees it."

"You're not jealous, John?" She looked wistful.

"Jenny, I feel the same about Diane. She comes into the room and I turn to jelly."

"John! Now I'm jealous!" And she was.

"I think that's how men feel about Diane, Jenny. She's just…well, forget it. But we wouldn't swap her for our wives. It's different. As you said, it's the silver screen, unreal. I shouldn't have said that, but you know what I mean." Jenny did know what he meant. The air cleared.

"Giles says we need bait, Jenny."

"I'm the bait, John. I know." John had wanted to keep Jenny out of this thing, but he knew that she was the key. He also knew that this was the best way to safeguard her for the future, but it still hurt. He did not want to take the risk, but he had to take the risk. He could not do this with Jenny alone. He needed Giles to help. He needed Ross to help plan what they should do. He could not do this on his own. It was too close to him.

"Before we do this, Jenny, I want you and me to spend a weekend away, just us, the two of us. I don't know about you, but I need that to go through with this." Jenny saw how the decision he had made was tearing him apart, and she agreed. Floating free in the current with Bill Hadley, she would need something to hold on to, she would need all the help he could give her, to escape the evil and the enchantment of that man. Foreboding, excitement, anxiety, it all mingled within her.

The first thing John did the next morning was to book flights to New York. He loved the wide-open spaces, but this time it had to be different. Then he left messages for Ross and Giles, explaining that he would be away for three days and asking that they get together, when he got back, as he put it, to bait the trap.

They landed at La Guardia and fought their way through the traffic to mid-town Manhattan. John told Jenny that they had no particular objective in mind. Just take it as it comes. They wandered down into Little Italy, finally succumbing to the earnest entreaties of a doorman to take lunch. They proceeded to eat cheap Italian crap at five times the price they were used to at Juanita's. They headed back up north and reached the Empire State Building. They thought they'd give it a go, not having done it before, and joined a massive line at the ticket office. Jenny scouted around while John waited, and established that the haze, smog, call it what you will, meant no views today. So they headed up further north instead. John suggested they book a room in the Roosevelt, but it was full, so they headed down south again.

The bustle began as office workers came out onto the street and the bars began to fill. It was fun and they moved through this for them alien world, populated by overdressed freaks from offices and underdressed weirdoes from god knows where. They had to laugh at the self-seriousness of this contorted existence. John tried a couple of hotels, eventually with success. The room probably should have cost in cents what it cost in dollars, but the bar was pleasant, old world pretence in the basement of a tower block, and they had a couple of beers. After the disaster of lunch, John suggested they be more circumspect for dinner. They ended up in somewhere called Jake's Steak House. Well, one can experience worse than sitting outside at midnight, consuming a twenty-two ounce steak. Several bars later, they made it back to the hotel, and in their hotel room made up for all the earlier deprivations of big city life.

John awoke in the dim morning, light filtering through net curtains, to see Jenny smiling at him. As he looked into her eyes, they both knew that they were leaving New York this morning. It had been worth a try, but the wide-open spaces beckoned. They knew where they wanted to be, and expectation made the struggle back to the airport bearable.

***

It was the familiar track up into the hills that John and Jenny chose to take. This time they would fork westwards up the smaller valley where it joined the stream they had followed last time. The climb was steep and the view was restricted to the narrow cleft of the valley, until finally clearing the trees, the wide expanse of the plain spread out below them. Here they decided to halt, exhausted by a solid four hour trek.

"New York, New York," John said softly, as he broke branches of deadwood for the fire, and Jenny gave a gentle laugh, sipping from a cool bottle of mineral water. As the fire took, John cracked open a couple of beers and handed one to Jenny. There was absolute silence, and then the fire began to spit and broke the spell. They lingered by the fire late into the night before finally extracting the sleeping bag to retire for the night, expectant of the climb to the head of the valley the next day.

The embers of the campfire glowed red. Leaves rustled in a soft breeze, and in the distance a coyote howled. In the first glimmers of dawn a cocoon beside the fire gradually took on the form of a dark green sleeping bag. From the west a bank of black cloud took up its battle formation against the light from the east, pushing back the growing light of dawn as it advanced with its deepening gloom. The first heavy drops signalled the attack and then the full force from the west poured down its deluge in torrents.

Even as John scrambled from the sleeping bag, pools of water were forming on the hard baked earth and rivulets formed on the slopes above. Jenny held out in the vain hope of warmth and continued slumber, but the bag was already sucking in the water and the cold. Dressing at dawn under a cold shower as the fire, the chance of breakfast, died was how they started the third day of their break. Soaked to the skin, before and after dressing, with no waterproof gear, they trudged back down the way they had come the previous afternoon. Their clothes were heavy with water and their shoes squelched with each step through the slippery mud. They slipped and skidded, splattering themselves with mud, down the slopes, steep on the way up, treacherous on the way down. Ill equipped as they were for this extraordinary storm, it chased them from the hills relentlessly.

Back at the car, they struggled into dry clothes and sat munching peanuts as the rain poured down on the windshield. It was still just nine a.m. on the third day of their pre-action break.

"Breakfast at the first place we pass on the road," John proposed.

"You got it," she replied.

Home by lunch, it seemed as if they had been away for more than a week and the New York experience seemed like ancient history. In retrospect the break had with all its trials turned out to exactly what they needed to develop the mental strength to launch into the whole Bill Hadley and Co. enterprise.

***

It rankled with Bob Mitchell that nothing had resulted from the letter that Bill had drafted for Jim to send to the woman, the special investigator. Bob decided he had better look into the matter himself. For a few days he hung around in the neighbour-hood of the police precinct. She must come and go to her place of work, take lunch maybe, he reasoned. He looked in stores, drank endless cups of coffee in fast food joints, and generally failed to get anywhere. After some days, he was on the point of giving up, when he saw her. She entered the building on the arm of a grey haired older guy, more family than business, Bob guessed.

After half-an-hour they came out together. Bob was sitting in his vehicle, ready to follow them. They climbed into a grey open Mercedes. Traffic was light, so he had no problem tracking them at an unobtrusive distance, only running one red light, and he probably would have done that anyway. The Merc headed out of downtown and soon they were in the leafy suburbs. It swung into the driveway of a brick built house, fronted with a porch and banks of massive white painted windows. Bob stopped fifty yards further on and strolled back towards the house, whistling. Outside the next but one house, a teenage kid displayed adolescent apathy as he hosed down his parents' Jaguar. Bob took a mighty kick at a coke can, lying on the sidewalk. It sailed over the Jaguar and dropped onto the manicured lawn thirty yards further on, just short of the grey Merc. The kid was impressed, but he didn't show it.

"They're not gonna like that," he said, squinting at Bob.

"You mean that tight little cunt, or her Dad?" Bob rolled his eyes in mock horror.

"The tight little cunt's the wife," the kid said.

Bob let out a low whistle. "Where do these guys get 'em?" And he walked on.

Bob's first thought was to have Jim Duggan break in with him, to check the house out, and he looked at the time, five thirty. They could do it tonight. Tie them up in bed, lock the kids in a room, if they had any, and trash the place. Then he remembered her quick reactions and violent response, when he had jerked her backwards over the sofa at his place. He decided on more conventional investigations first. He would save the fun for later. There was already a question mark developing in his mind. A stunning number like this one, living in a place like this, with an obviously wealthy husband – what's she doing with the police. Step one: let's find out who this guy is. He took down the address and returned to his vehicle.

Bob spent a day on the problem, unsuccessfully. He didn't want to ask the neighbours. He thought about the mailbox, but that was locked. Finally, on the second day he tracked Giles to his place of work. Giles disappeared into the building, but it was simple enough to quiz the porter and learn what he needed to know.

The knowledge that the special investigator was the wife of a local psychiatrist disturbed Bob Mitchell sufficiently to prompt him to get his brain checked out. He would see what he could find out. He registered with Giles as Mitchell Roberts, who was suffering from headaches and sleepless nights and got an appointment for the next day.

The psychiatric session was routine, mostly to do with his habits, diet, medication and so on. It looked like it would take a few sessions to deal with the headaches. Mitchell was thinking about the fees, which would be enough to give him a real headache, when Giles excused himself and left the room for a couple of minutes. Why he should do this was a mystery to Mitchell, but he jumped at the chance to take a look around and see if he could find out anything useful. Rifling through papers on Giles' desk, he came upon a card addressed in Giles' hand to Diane, but otherwise blank, uncompleted. Using the reasoning that you never know what may come in handy when, he slipped the card into his pocket. He tried the grey steel cabinets, but they were locked. Otherwise there were heavy tomes on psychology and clinical psychiatry. All in all Mitchell thought he had drawn a blank. He sat down and waited for Giles to return. Giles suggested another session and Mitchell agreed that he would give a call as soon as he was more definite about his schedule. After Mitchell Roberts left Giles was mystified that he could not find the note he had started to write to Diane. He was sure he had been about to write it when Roberts came in.

The grain of suspicion grew within Bob Mitchell. Bill seemed so smug that his plan was running smoothly, yet what was going on here? He decided that further surveillance was necessary. He thought he should concentrate on the psychiatrist. He would be easier to track than the wife. Bob knew the co-ordinates of both home and office, so he just needed to work out the routine and then watch for anything out of the ordinary. The wife would be more difficult, because he had no idea of what she was up to, where she went or what she did. Certainly the police precinct figured surprisingly little in her role as special investigator. Over a couple of days, he established that Giles was either in his consultancy or at the hospital. Few patients came to see him, but then if he charged them what he had charged Bill, he would not need many madmen to make a respectable fortune.

On the afternoon of the third day, Bob followed the grey Merc back from the consultancy to the house. Well that's it, he thought, a short day. Bob drove on up the road and turned to head back down the street for home. Then he noticed, as he passed the Merc, that the psychiatrist had not got out of the Merc. He looked in his rear-view mirror, saw the house door open, and the wife came out. Bob pulled over. He waited for them to pass and then pulled out to follow at a distance. They headed for the town centre and were soon on Main Street passing Bob's favourite bank. They continued a few blocks and turned left. A few hundred yards further and then they stopped right outside the apartment block where Bob had snatched the Ralphs woman. Jesus, he thought, swung into the side street and parked. He jumped out of the car and raced around the corner to see them entering the building. He told himself that he had to be sure, and cautiously followed. As they entered the lift, Bob crossed to the stairwell. He leapt up the stairs. He heard the lift stop, its doors open, and then the ring of a bell. Bob heard her voice as she greeted them, the voice of the hostage, of the Ralphs woman. He stopped where he was on the stairs. Bill

Hadley, Bob muttered under his breath, it stretches even my credulity that the special investigator makes a social call with her husband on the prime suspect and his wife. His long low whistle echoed in the stairwell.

I think I found out what I need to know, Bob thought, as he returned to his car. Driving out of town he thought it over. Bill thinks his clever plan is humming along. Meanwhile, these people are playing their own little game. Cat and mouse? Where does that leave me? If I tell Bill, what will he do? Start some other crazy plan? Fiddle around on his planogram? What a joke. Whatever he does he will want to be in control. But he's screwed up this time, so do I want to risk it a second time. I'll think this over. We meet tomorrow evening, so let's mull it over until then. Maybe it's my turn to take charge now, to play my cards close to my chest.

The next day Bob decided to move his personal surveillance to the Ralphs woman. For much of the morning this meant hanging around in sight of her apartment block. Then what Bob saw made a major decision for him, the decision about what he should tell Bill Hadley, if anything. What Bob saw was that Bill Hadley met the Ralphs woman for lunch at Juanita's. If Bob was sure of one thing, it was that Bill would not mention the meeting when they came together that same evening. Bob, he told himself, you sure did the right move in deciding to take your own measures to look after number one. Bob Mitchell comes first. Period.

As Jenny walked up to Juanita's, Bill climbed out of his truck where he had been waiting. Greeting her, he failed to see Bob drive by with a vicious smirk on his face. Jenny was bouncy and alive, exuberant that she was at last doing something, and safe with the assurance of the group last night that for the time-being there was no personal threat to her from Bill Hadley. If the suggestion of lunch had surprised him, he had not shown it on the phone. And now they were there. Act Three, Scene One, Take One, she thought to herself, as she smiled at Bill in greeting. Camera.

Juanita's was in its usual high activity. Broad windows gave on the street, lightly curtained. The tables were set back in clusters with bright checked lunchtime table clothes. Formal linen was reserved for the evening. Most of the tables were full. Jenny headed for a table for three in the corner, explaining that John would join them for coffee, when he was free later. Jenny gave Diane a friendly waive, seated near the bar with a group of ladies.

The plan they had discussed the previous day was that Jenny would try to get closer to Hadley, which should not be difficult, given his evident interest in her. She would then begin to expose to Hadley fault lines developing in her relationship with John, fault lines caused by his suspension from the police and the threat it represented to him. The idea was to draw Hadley out into the open, to play upon his weakness, and then trap him into making a wrong move, or into disclosing something compromising to him.

Bill immediately took the ordering in hand, and, having dismissed the waitress, began to probe Jenny gently about her background and how she came to live in the locality, as she was obviously not local. He then moved on to her aspirations in life, and she found herself gaily chatting about her plans, in just the same way as she had talked during the walks in the woods as a hostage. The similarity struck her, as she spoke, and somehow she wanted Bill to know that she knew. She thought she saw recognition, a knowing look behind his gaze, and she felt him draw her towards him. She was suddenly glad of Diane's presence across the restaurant, and of the familiar surroundings, which gave her stability, protection. She had to release herself from his power, to get him to speak now. It sounded so false as she put the same questions about his background to him, but he seemed relaxed.

"I'm on the verge of taking the next major step in my life, Jenny." He was moving on now to his aspirations.

"How so?"

"An organisation. I've been working mama and papa style, really. Now I'm going to build a real organisation." He saw no harm in telling her. He was not going to tell her it was to be a mafia style organisation.

"That sounds ambitious." She felt a little flattery was in order here.

"I have the means now. I have the will. And, you know, I'm a planner, and organiser, a strategist, not a doer." He looked at her questioningly.

"I'm a doer, Bill. All natural bounce and action. That's me."

"Jenny," he laughed, "just the sort I'm going to need. What about John? Tell him to give up the police." She looked darkly, but said nothing. "Just the skills I need," he continued, amused by the real meaning of what he said. A corrupt cop would be perfect, but not this one. He was heading straight for jail, without passing Go. Maximum sentence with his record. He saw Jenny giving him a quizzical look.

"Leave John and come with me," he said. She was startled. "Just a joke, Jenny." He laughed winningly and she joined in. He had not been able to resist testing her reaction, and liked what he had seen. Through the main course he unfolded his picture of what an organisation should be like and how he should motivate his men, and women. He truly is an imaginative guy, she thought, and very charismatic. It was Bill who spotted John come in.

"Hey, John. Over here." John came across. He did feel like an intruder, and though not an actor by nature, he slotted into the part he had to play perfectly. He was morose, uncommunicative and clearly in the habit of giving Jenny a hard time, taking his grievances out on her. In the end, Bill was glad when coffee was finished and he could take his leave.

"Jenny, thank you. John, that was really great fun. Let's do this more often. You know what, come out shooting on the truck." His thoughts were not what he spoke – Jesus, this guy's doing my work for me; he's driving her round the twist with his petty little problems.

After Bill had left, Diane came over.

"Well?"

"Perfect," John was laughing. "He thinks I'm a real bastard, and

I loved every moment."

"Nothing new. All men are bastards, John." Diane sat down in Bill's place.

"He's got major plans. He told me about them." Jenny thought back to the conversation and Bill's enthusiasm for his organisation.

"What plans?" John enquired.

"Since I don't know any better, I have to assume he thinks he's going to be…" Her voice tailed off.

"To be what?" Diane asked.

"I suppose…I suppose it has to be Al Capone, since he's not Sicilian."

CHAPTER FIFTEEN

As evening drew in, the farmhouse stood gaunt against the surrounding trees. The clouds massed, the strength of the wind grew steadily and then the storm broke, the second in a week. Inside Bill Hadley sat in a pool of light, thrown by his desk light, hunched over his laptop. Jim Duggan occupied the seats in front of the fireplace, gripping his second can of beer. Outside the wind howled and the patter of rain developed into a roar. Lightning flashed, followed by a peal of thunder. Bill continued to tap away at the machine. The lights flickered and recovered. The front door crashed open and then slammed shut. Bob Mitchell stepped in from the hall, shaking off the water like a dog. He slung his green hunter's jacket back into the hall onto the stone floor.

"Any news, guys?" he boomed as he stepped into the room, thinking, your last chance to come clean with me, Bill. Come on, Bill. Juanita's? Broads? He was answered by a weary silence, in this case very expressive in his view. The next party to be the target of my surveillance talents is you, Bill, he promised himself, and chuckled aloud.

"What's the joke, Bob?" Jim asked.

"You're the joke, Jim." He bellowed with laughter at this joke, which did not amuse Jim, but then Bob's witticisms seldom did. The lights flickered, again recovered and failed. The room was faintly lit by the glow of Bill's laptop, now on battery power. Bill continued to type. With a reluctant sigh, Bob felt his way into the hall and extracted a couple of camping lights from a cupboard, the sort that function when you unscrew the top. A halloween green now lit the room. Jim struck a match and flicked it into the fireplace. The dry wood sparked, caught and flamed. A flickering yellow joined the Halloween green.

"When shall we three meet again," Jim cackled, " In thund…"

"We are meeting, you idiot," Bob interrupted. "Get off your machine, Bill, and get your arse over here."

"Sorry, just sending my mom an email. Asking her if I can bring these two nice guys home, I just met. OK, OK, I'm coming. Cool it."

As Bill brought them up to speed on how he saw his plan developing, omitting the bit about Jenny, the private bit, Bob listened with detachment. This guy really does not know, Bob thought. He's lost the plot, and I am not telling him; not about who the blonde girl is, nor about her meeting with the Ralphs. From now on I take control of my life. I'll step in when the time's right.

The entry bell went, and Bill crossed into the hall. He came back in followed by two females underdressed, overmade-up, underdeveloped intellects, overdeveloped busts. Bob stood up and moved across the room, in the greenish flickering light. He stood in front of the tall blonde woman ran his hands down her sides, tracing the outline of her figure.

"Your choice next, Jim." Bob laughed, eyeing the sleazy brunette in a tight red dress and thigh-length boots.

"I'm not exclusive," she said, looking across at Jim. "Depends on you guys. Two suits me. We'll take whatever you've got." A thin, nervous laugh belied her bravado.

"Bill, you dreaming of your little Jenny?" Jim taunted, realising why there were just two whores tonight. Bill contained the psychological explosion this triggered, but not the physiological one as his face turned red and his limbs quivered with rage. It took half a minute to pass, and he turned back to his laptop. Jim set about pouring a couple of drinks from the cocktail cabinet, but Bob took his number straight through into the guest room.

"I've seen you before," Bob said.

"Seen? Hmm, I remember you as the guy with the firehose stuffed down his pants."

"Don't they educate you girls? Like how to talk nice." Bob unbottoned her blouse from the neck down.

"Only it was like some jerk filled the water tank with kerosene," she continued regardless. "Like you wanna put out my fire with jet fuel." Bob was beginning to enjoy the direction the conversation was taking as his hands moved down to the zip of her skirt, and she released his pants.

"This time, lady, I'm gonna use the afterburners," he growled.

"This time," she laughed, grappling him to the floor, "I'm Saint George slaying the dragon." Rolling on top of him, she joined battle, narrating the story as she went. "I clasp my trusty lance. Firm in my hands, I grip it with my thighs and thrust down on the beast. My lance drives deep into the beast's belly." Bob was panting by now. "I thrust again and again. The beast struggles, it moans, will it not die? I thrust again." But the dragon was more powerful than Saint George anticipated. It rolled over and picked Saint George up with it. Now the dragon was banging Saint George rhythmically against the door to the lounge.

"Jesus Christ! What the hell's going on in there?" The brunette was visibly scared by the crashing, moaning and screaming from the next room. "Take me upstairs, Jim. Keep me away from that maniac." She chose her expletives appropriately. As the noise abated, Bill switched of the cassette recorder. I'll play that back to them when we want a good laugh sometime, he thought. After a couple of minutes, St George emerged, naked, and made for the front door, saying she wanted to cool off and loved storms. Bob, being more prudish, came out in his underpants, and settled for the bourbon bottle in preference to the storm. Then he told Bill he wanted some spectator sport and headed upstairs.

Meanwhile, Bill tapped away on the planogram. After ten minutes Saint George reappeared from outside with water streaming from her hair and body, which glowed in the flickering green light. Then the power came back on. Bill blinked in the bright light, and saw a naked Jenny shimmering before him. As he reached out towards her, his eyes adjusted to the light and reality reasserted itself. He turned back to his laptop and planned further. Bewildered by his behaviour, she turned to the cocktail cabinet and poured herself a drink. She turned off the lights apart from one table lamp and relaxed, naked and still dripping wet, infront of the fire. She threw on a couple more logs. From the noises up above, it was evident that Bob had relinquished his role as mere spectator. Unless she was asked, she would not join in. And if she was asked? Well, it was a good living.

Some minutes later Jim and Bob came down the stairs, singing Clementine off-key. Bill typed away, and the blonde decided it was time to dress. The brunette came down the stairs, looking as if she needed a new outfit. The two women left wordlessly. Home visits were always paid for in cash in advance, and Bill, good customer that he was, was no exception to that rule.

Bob's spirits were revived. It was still before midnight, so he told Jim that he had worked out where his blonde assailant, the special investigator, lived, and suggested they go over there and have some fun. Jim was about to agree, but then watching Bob gulp down another half tumbler of bourbon, he took the view that it was the bourbon speaking. He took the tactful way out and suggested that they have another couple of drinks first. By the time Bill turned off his laptop forty-five minutes later, the other two were both snoring infront of the fire.

***

Giles was amazed, as he debriefed Jenny on the lunch with Hadley at Juanita's. It was as if Hadley had thrown caution to the wind: that he should hint at her joining him; that, even in jest, he should hint at her leaving John for him. *Many a true word is spoken in jest* may be apt for all of us, he opined, but for the type of psychopath we believe Hadley to be it is highly revealing.

"He believes he's closing in, Jenny," Giles said. He looked at

John and Diane. "We have to move now. Invite him in for the kill, while his vision is blurred.

"How?" Diane asked. Giles was pensive, and then finally he brought himself to express his thoughts.

"We need to stage a scene. Have Jenny break down. Draw him in."

"But what are we looking for?" John asked. "We need hard evidence. How will Jenny get that?" The phone rang. Since John chaired their discussions these days, as senior policeman, Jenny left the kitchen to answer it. She came back into the kitchen, flustered.

"It was Hadley," she said. "He wants to see me this afternoon. I just kind of winged it. I agreed. To be honest I didn't know how to say, no." She looked at them, distraught.

"Jenny, you did right," John stated.

"You did," Giles agreed. "See what he says and then we'll reconvene."

"I'll come with you, Jenny," Diane said. "Let's play this safe...for once."

Diane's offer and Jenny's acceptance changed the course of events. When Mitchell, tailing Hadley, saw the three of them together, Hadley, the special investigator and the Ralphs girl, his cool snapped. He rammed his foot down on the throttle, tyres screaming as he rounded the corner. All three of them started and looked round, but Mitchell's vehicle was gone.

The surveillance on Bill Hadley had proved successful beyond measure. It was now clear to Bob Mitchell that the man was out of control and a liability. Not only that but in Mitchell's eyes it appeared that the Ralph's camp was closing in on Hadley. This meant that they were in turn closing in on him, Mitchell. The second thing that was clear was that Hadley was proceeding with his plans for the organisation, despite his and Duggan's vehement objections. Even if the Ralphs crowd failed to pull anything off – and Mitchell could not really see what they could realistically achieve – he and Duggan were still stuck with the problem that facts incriminating to them would be revealed to other organisation members. Even if it was only the fact of their existence, that was still a threat. This neither he nor Duggan would tolerate. Hadley's recent real estate interests had aroused Mitchell's suspicions. He just needed to confirm these suspicions, and then, if they proved correct, he would go ahead and take them all out, every single one of them, in one fell swoop.

Mitchell called Hadley on the phone. He explained that he had had second thoughts about the organisation. Hadley was right. How was he, Mitchell, to exploit his talents if they continued to work on their own? Let the flunkies do the groundwork was the way he was thinking now, and let him, Mitchell, move in for the kill. Likewise, they should use Duggan for his specialist skills. Hadley was surprised by the change of heart, but then in the back of his mind he had always known that he would win through. His was the sensible, the rational way.

"Look, I have made some progress, Bob," Hadley explained.

"Great. What do we do?" Mitchell asked.

"Bring Duggan with you tomorrow. I'll get there at four. Number Five, Hunter's view. Got that?"

"Got it. Westside. Right? We'll be there. Four sharp. Why there?" Mitchell waited for the answer, which came after the pause.

"Surprise, Bob. Just a little surprise."

So I have guessed right, Mitchell thought, as he replaced the receiver.

***

Bob stopped his car beside a hedge.

"You know what that is?" he asked Jim, pointing at a two storey building, surrounded by its own lawns, edged with woods.

"This is a 1980's building with no architectural merit, badly designed so that you can see into all the rooms right here from the road." Jim surveyed the building and its surrounds.

"That's our HQ." Jim boomed, broadcasting the fact far and wide. "Bill has bought this place for his organisation."

"We don't want an organisation," Jim screeched, manifestly upset.

"He's lost it, Jim."

"So what do we do?"

"I've done it." Bob started the car and drove round to the entrance, parking by the front door. "Bill wants to see us, right? Well, it's here. This is where he told me to bring you." Bob looked at Jim.

"Why?" Jim's nerves were rattled.

"Because he's done it without telling us. He wants an organisation, because he thinks he's Napoleon. Right?" Bob gave a low chuckle.

"OK." Jim acquiesced.

"Come inside with me," Bob suggested, and Jim used his skill as a locksmith to make that possible. They ascended the stairs to the floor above. Bill led Jim into a smartly furnished room.

"This is where we meet," Bob said. "The reason I know that is the room's furnished."

"Makes sense," Jim said.

"If you agree, Jim, I'm gonna take them all out." Bob turned to Jim and waited for his answer.

"If there's an organisation, today or tomorrow, taking them out is fine by me," Jim replied without hesitation.

Bob went on to explain his plan, which was very simple: Bill and every one else who knew anything about anything would be shot here in this very house. After that, he and Jim would leave. Go and do their thing elsewhere. The point was, Bob explained, that Bill had tied himself up in this whole thing about incriminating John Ralphs, and that was bad news. There were too many loose ends.

So how come everyone who needed to be shot would be here, Jim wondered. That was also simple, according to Bob. Bill would be here because he had invited them, Bob and Jim. The police, including Ralphs, would be here because Bob had indirectly and discretely tipped them off that this was the opportunity for surveillance, and more, of Bill. Jim had questioned why that would make them good targets, as in people who get shot, and Bob had laughed. He took Jim through into the room across the landing. The room was unfurnished but for two chairs. "Two wives, will sit here," Bob said. "To the minute, they will stand up and walk into the other room, where we will be with Bill. The police outside will rush in, when they see the women at risk, and then it's down to me, Jim, and you've seen me in action. Boom, boom, boom."

"I don't understand why the women will do that, Bob." Jim was looking around the room for a clue.

"Because they have precise instructions. Only they think they come from this psychiatrist and not from me. Right? It's all fixed up, Jim. This is it. Trust me."

"I agree. What would you have done if I didn't agree, since you've got it all fixed up?"

"Shoot you." Bill was as pragmatic as ever.

Jim decided he had made a wise choice.

"Come on, Jim. Let's go. The women will be here in half-an-hour. Leave the door unlocked for them."

Diane was already on her way to pick up Jenny, exactly according to the schedule set out in her instructions. Jenny came down from her office on time. She had received Diane's message that she should be there.

"Hi, Diane. How are you doing? Looking good. What is all this? Fill me in."

"This is weird," Diane said to Jenny. "After Giles left, I got this note from him. Very specific instructions. She showed Jenny a typed sheet of paper folded into a card addressed to her in Giles' hand. We're supposed to go and hide in this place and then come out exactly when he says. Maybe we're reconvening like he said yesterday."

"Sounds like John," Jenny said. "Police work. He probably

suggested it to Giles."

"Well, everything's here, right down to the address of the place, floor-layout and the timing. Let's go. If you say so, Jenny, let's go."

"I say so." Jenny laughed and gestured to Diane's car. They chatted in the car on the way to the rendezvous. On the one hand, they were relieved that something was finally about to happen, while on the other hand, they both felt first night nerves. Both of them thought the instructions were strange, but these concerns were set at rest, when they arrived at the building. Sure enough, everything was exactly as described. They made their way up the stairs, and located the room where they were apparently to wait in secret. Diane turned the key in the lock behind them, and they sat down, trying to suppress initial giggles at the incongruity of it all.

***

Spotting the police car slip in behind the trees, Bill turned from the window to Bob and Jim.

"What the hell are the police doing here?" Bill lost his normal cool. He saw that Bob was looking smug.

"It's the final bloodbath, Bill. You screwed up. I'm fixing it." Bob leered at him.

"Fixing what?"

"Calm down, Bill. I've got their wives. Any moment now, I'm taking them out one by one."

"You've what?"

"They think the psychiatrist sent them here. In exactly one minute, wife number one will walk in here, followed by wife number two. And guess what? They'll see little old me, waiting. Bang, bang. Remember: no one lives to tell the tale."

Looking up at the building from his hiding place across the lawn, John saw a figure come into view in the window of the landing outside the room where he was observing Hadley. It was Jenny. What the hell was Jenny doing there? His heart stopped. Jenny walked though the doorway into the room and stopped dead. Standing square in front of her was Bob Mitchell. Realising what was happening, John wanted to scream out a warning, but he knew it was to no avail, too late. Through the window of the room he saw Mitchell slowly raise his gun arm and fix his aim on Jenny, taking his time. John could not bear to look. He covered his face in his hands and three shots rang out. John slumped to the ground sobbing.

It was not Mitchell's shots that John heard. Hadley felt himself watching in slow motion as he saw Mitchell raise his pistol. He saw Jenny stricken with shock. Bob had to do this, he knew, but feelings welled up inside him that he had never felt before, as rage at Bob and longing for Jenny combined like a volatile chemical reaction. His reflexes possessed him. He drew his automatic, firing three rapid shots into the back of Mitchell's head. In that instant Diane shot through the door behind Jenny and was on top of Hadley. She pinned him to the floor and screamed for help. Duggan scrambled clear, diving through the closed window in a shower of broken glass. Dropping one storey down onto the lawn below, he rolled over and was on his feet, running for the car. With a screech of tyres he was gone.

Ross was screaming at John that Jenny was OK and to get in there. John looked up in disbelief to see Jenny through the window, moving slowly forward. He leapt the fence and raced across the lawn, realising this is what he should have done anyway when he froze at the sight of Jenny confronted by Mitchell. Ross was already through the door and taking the stairs three at a time. He burst into the room to see Hadley on the floor, Diane crouching over him with a knee in his back. He was choking and spitting blood. He would only ever speak again in a whisper: she had smashed his larynx, resisting arrest as it was later claimed. As for Duggan, he was never seen again.

The Herald and Courier

HOMICIDE: AND AN END TO TERROR?

Yesterday afternoon the police made an arrest for homicide. William Hadley stands accused of the murder of Robert Mitchell, both residents of our county.

We understand from police sources that Hadley had been sought for questioning in connection with the bank raids that have blighted our town in recent weeks. Progress in investigations had led them to Hadley, already questioned earlier in the investigation.

It was while the police sought to take in Hadley for questioning that he gunned down Mr Mitchell in cold blood. The police are not aware of the motive for this shooting, but they witnessed it, catching Hadley redhanded, as they entered a building in search of Hadley.

We speculate that Hadley's arrest may have brought to an end the reign of terror under which we have lived these last months.

THE END

OTHER BOOKS AVAILABLE FROM
TWENTY FIRST CENTURY PUBLISHERS LTD

RAMONA

How did a little girl come to be abandoned in the orange scented square of the Andalusian City of Seville? Find out, when the course of her life is resumed at age seventeen.

"Ramona" is a literary work that deals with Europe in transition and the relationships that form an ususual life.

Ramona by Johnny John Heinz
ISBN: 1-904433-01-4

MEANS TO AN END

Enter the world of money laundering, financial manipulation and greed, where a shadowy middle eastern organisation takes on a major corporation in the US. As the action shifts through exotic locations, who wins out in the end? Certainly, the author's first hand experience of international finance lends the plot chilling credibility.

Means to an End by Johnny John Heinz
ISBN: 1-84375-008-2

TARNISHED COPPER

Tarnished Copper is a story of greed, deception and corruption in one of the most volatile of financial markets. The author, Geoffrey Sambrook, has been a metal trader for 20 years, seeing the collapse of the International Tin Council, the Sumitomo Affair and numerous other market shenanigans, and brings an insider's unique insight into the way markets can be manipulated for profit. The fictional characters of Tarnished Copper seem horrifyingly real as they follow their dance of deception, culminating in untold riches for some, and death for another. A new, cerebral voice in financial fiction.

Tarnished Copper by Geoffrey Sambrook
ISBN 1-904433-02-2

Visit our website: www.twentyfirstcenturypublishers.com

Printed in the United Kingdom
by Lightning Source UK Ltd.
9387400001B

9 781904 433002